A TASTE
OF ROMANCE

Other books by Roni Denholtz:

Lights of Love
Negotiating Love
Salsa with Me
Somebody to Love
Marquis in a Minute

A TASTE
OF ROMANCE

•

Roni Denholtz

AVALON BOOKS

NEW YORK

Published by Avalon Books, an imprint of
Thomas Bouregy & Co., Inc.
160 Madison Avenue, New York, NY 10016

Library of Congress Cataloging-in-Publication Data

Denholtz, Roni S.
    A taste of romance / Roni Denholtz.
        p. cm.
    ISBN 978-0-8034-7792-6 (acid-free paper)
    1. Television cooking shows—Fiction.
    2. Man-woman relationships—Fiction.   I. Title.
    PS3554.E5314T38 2010
    813'.54—dc22
                                    2010018142

PRINTED IN THE UNITED STATES OF AMERICA
ON ACID-FREE PAPER
BY HADDON CRAFTSMEN, BLOOMSBURG, PENNSYLVANIA

For my sister,
Debbie Paitchel Klein,
with love

Acknowledgments

My sincere thanks to Debbie Paitchel Klein for the information about TV productions and Jalal Shamsey for the information about electricians.

Chapter One

"This is one of my boyfriend's favorite dishes," Nicole Vitarelli said, smiling at the camera.

Yeah, my imaginary boyfriend, she thought.

"You can see how beautiful the Chicken Cordon Bleu looks when it's finished," she continued. One of the cameras moved in to get a close-up of the main course. "That wasn't too hard, was it? And it's so delicious."

She automatically added a scoop of lemon rice to the plate, then spooned on some plain green peas. "Here's how the whole meal looks together." She brought the dishes over to the table, which was already set with fine china and sparkling crystal goblets. She kept her hands steady as she proceeded to light two red candles on the table.

"Now you're all ready for your romantic dinner. Enjoy it, and please join me in two weeks for another episode of *A Taste of Romance!* I'll be sharing my grandmother's secret recipe for lasagna." She continued to smile as the cameraman slowly backed up and got a wide shot of her with the food in the studio's kitchen.

1

"Cut! Very good, Nicole—I think that's it."

Nicole relaxed her smile and posture. As much as she enjoyed taping the show, it was always a relief when it was over and she didn't have to perform and be quite so perky. She sat on the kitchen stool as Irene Abrams, the show's producer, came toward her.

The two camera people backed up, and someone switched off the brightest lights and put on the regular lights in the studio. She immediately felt the change in temperature as the room cooled.

Taping this show had gone pretty smoothly, and they hadn't had to do more than a couple of retakes. Nicole smiled at Irene as she approached, satisfied that this episode of her show would be easy to edit.

As she got a look at Irene's face, however, she felt a twinge of uneasiness. Irene looked perturbed. The curly-haired woman was in her fifties and usually wore a happy expression—but today her expression was different.

"Nicole, do you have a minute?" Irene asked.

"Of course," Nicole replied.

"Come on over to my office."

Nicole followed Irene, wondering what this was about. Her show had been well received since it had begun airing almost six months ago. She didn't think it would be cancelled. Then what could it be? Were they going to change the time it aired?

She'd first met her producer when Irene had taken the Italian cooking class Nicole taught one night a week at her community school adult class.

After the six-week class ended, Irene, a producer at the local cable TV station, had told Nicole they were going to try doing a few cooking shows on a rotating basis. "They're so popular now," she'd said, "and our executive producer wants to try something new. We have advertisers already interested in the idea." Irene had said that they wanted to do one of the shows on the theme of "Romantic Dinners." Her boss, Thomas Clarkson, the executive producer, had asked her to find a young, attractive, enthusiastic woman who knew how to cook to host the show. "I immediately thought of you!" Irene had said.

Nicole had auditioned and been accepted, and the show, which aired every other week, had quickly become a success. Over the last few months she'd gotten friendly with Irene. As she slid into the chair by Irene's desk, Nicole now wondered what was on the producer's mind. She took a deep breath. Even in here, she could smell the delectable Chicken Cordon Bleu with its ham-and-Swiss-cheese filling.

Irene sat down, a slight frown marring her otherwise-pleasant face. She glanced out the window, and Nicole followed her gaze. The September evening was warm, and the windows were closed to let the air conditioned air circulate. There were starkly beautiful pink streaks in the sky as the sun moved toward sunset.

"What's up?" Nicole asked lightly, trying to ignore the strange sensation in her stomach. What was wrong?

Irene sighed and looked at Nicole. "I guess this is . . . kind of my fault. You know how I suggested a few months ago that you mention your boyfriend once or twice on each show, since it's about romantic dinners?"

"Yes . . . ," Nicole said slowly. She had complied, although Irene knew she wasn't dating anyone special right now, and hadn't dated anyone special for a long time. Her boyfriend was pure fiction.

Irene sighed again. "Thomas wants your boyfriend to put in a guest appearance on the show."

Nicole felt her stomach plunge to the floor. "He what?" She stared at Irene as astonishment and consternation swept through her. "But I don't have—"

"—a boyfriend. I know you don't have a boyfriend," Irene said. She met Nicole's look straight on, her face flushing guiltily. "I feel bad. Your 'boyfriend' was my idea. But . . . you're going to have to come up with one—fast."

Nicole's stomach churned. *Where was she going to find a boyfriend?*

Chapter Two

S₀ who am I going to find to play the part of my boyfriend?" Nicole groaned to her sister that night.

Marla plopped down on the couch beside her. As soon as Nicole had gotten back to the house they rented together, Marla had recognized Nicole's distress and suggested that they both get into their pj's and relax with some ice cream and girl talk.

Nicole regarded her now. Marla was twenty-five, three years younger than Nicole, but they'd always been close. Marla was a nurse working with premature babies at a nearby hospital, and Nicole's full-time job was as an English teacher at a nearby middle school. They'd been tired of renting apartments in noisy complexes and had rented this house together. Marla worked a lot of the afternoon and evening shifts, so they didn't see each other every day, but this Friday evening they were both at home.

Nicole had racked her brain without success on the way back. She needed her sister's advice.

"Well, let's think about the guys you know," Marla

urged, dipping her spoon into her cookies-and-cream ice cream. "What about your friend Ben from work?"

Ben was a math teacher whom Nicole had known for a few years, but had always regarded simply as a friend. "No, he just started dating someone and I think it's going strong." She scooped up a spoonful of cherry vanilla, her favorite.

"Hmm . . . what about Tony? He's so cute."

"Our *cousin*?" Nicole frowned. Tony was cute, but she didn't want her cousin playing the part of her boyfriend! "Someone would be sure to find out we're related."

"You're probably right." Marla paused, looking thoughtful. "What about—what's his name—that guy next door you were friendly with in high school, the one who's a year younger?"

"Dave? No, I heard he just got engaged," Nicole said. She'd already gone through a bunch of names in her mind, ever since she'd left the TV studio, including the names Marla was mentioning now—with the exception of their cousin. She'd rejected every person she'd considered. "I thought of Patrick, and Darren, and Tyler"—all guys she had known in college—"but they don't live around here. And don't even think of suggesting Brad."

"I wouldn't!" Marla protested at the mention of Nicole's former boyfriend—the guy who had broken her heart.

Nicole scooched further down on the couch. She reeled off names of a couple of guys she'd dated in the last year—guys for whom she felt no particular feelings. "Jordan moved to Alaska, Sam went to Texas, and Harry—well, he's just kind of nerdy. He wouldn't look the part of anyone's boyfriend."

"Hmm, yeah, but what about—who's around here? Did

we meet anyone at the Labor Day barbecue?" Suddenly Marla's eyes widened.

Nicole regarded her sister. It sometimes felt like looking in a mirror. They both shared the same black hair and classic features, although Marla was an inch taller than Nicole's five feet four inches, and Marla had blue-gray eyes instead of Nicole's dark brown ones.

"What?" Nicole asked.

"How about that nice electrician from across the street—the one I met at the barbecue and asked to come over tomorrow and replace the chandelier? He's a good-looking guy."

Yes, he was. Even though she'd only seen him from a distance, Nicole had observed that he was cute, with a friendly smile.

The block they lived on had held a Labor Day barbecue at the Reynolds', neighbors who lived closest to the lake. Nicole had left early, since school started the following day. Between teaching tasks and unpacking—she and Marla had moved into their rental house only two days before—she'd had loads of stuff to do. Marla had stayed an hour longer, and returned home saying she'd met their neighbor across the street—and that he was an electrician. "That's just what we need!" she'd added. "His name's Jeremy. I asked him about the light fixture."

The following day Nicole had seen him with a short blond woman, coming out of his house, and the young woman had been carrying one of those pop-up hampers. Nicole had figured she was his girlfriend or fiancée.

"Remember, I think he's got a girlfriend," she reminded Marla. "It's too bad. He'd look good on TV."

"Well, when I spoke to him about the chandelier

yesterday, I didn't notice a wedding ring," Marla declared, licking her spoon. "I think he's about your age, or a little older."

The window air conditioner clicked on and began humming.

"That doesn't mean he doesn't have a significant other," Nicole pointed out.

"Hmm," Marla said, "maybe we'll be able to find out somehow."

"No." Nicole scooped up more ice cream. "I'll think of someone. I told Irene I'd try and figure out something over the weekend. I'll find someone who owes me a favor to play the role."

As she ate the sweet cherry-filled ice cream, she wished she felt as confident as she sounded. Who on earth could she ask to play the part of her boyfriend?

Jeremy slung his bag over his shoulder and proceeded to the small house across the street.

One of the sisters who lived there had called the other day, asking if he could replace the old, dilapidated dining room light fixture with a new one. Their landlord had said if they bought a new fixture he'd pay to have it installed safely.

The late-summer weather was warm but not uncomfortable, and increasing clouds were starting to block the sun. They'd probably get rain later. But this was his only appointment today, so by afternoon he'd probably be able to get his boat out on the lake.

He glanced back at his home. It wasn't huge, but it was probably larger than most single guys needed. He'd gotten a good deal on it the previous year, and he and his buddies had done a lot of work to fix it up.

He heard footsteps within seconds after he knocked, and then the door swung open.

"Come on in."

He'd met Marla, one of the two sisters who were renting the house, briefly at the Reynolds' annual Labor Day party. As he entered the living room, another young woman, who looked almost identical to her sister, came out of the kitchen at the back of the house. Both wore jeans and T-shirts—and both were gorgeous.

"You're twins?" he guessed.

The shorter one, the one who'd come out of the kitchen, shook her head but smiled. "No. We are sisters, though. I'm Nicole, and you've met Marla."

Nicole's smile was engaging, and ramped up her attractiveness. She would turn anyone's head—even his.

"I, ah, have to get ready for work," the one named Marla said. Close up, he could see there were subtle differences between the two. Marla had bluish-gray eyes and was slightly taller. She also looked a little more sophisticated—or maybe it was her expression, which was friendly, but appraising.

Nicole's expression, though, was pure sunshine. Her eyes were a deep chocolate brown, and seemed to smile along with her mouth.

"Marla's a nurse and she works some weekends," Nicole explained, turning back to him. "Now, here's the problem." She waved in the direction of a light fixture he'd spotted the moment he walked in.

Farther back from the living room was the dining room, which held a good-sized table. The chandelier over the table was decidedly old and hung crookedly.

"That is a problem. The wiring's probably ancient," he said. He put down his bag and grabbed some tools as Marla went upstairs. He examined the fixture and its wires. "I'll have to turn off the circuit breaker for a few minutes," he said.

"Oh, sure. I'll show you where it is. Want a soda?" Nicole offered.

"No thanks."

She called up to her sister that he was turning off some of the power. He followed her down to the basement, unable to stop from appreciating her figure as she moved ahead of him. She was curvy but trim—definitely the kind of woman who any guy would notice, even in her jeans and simple yellow T-shirt. He could smell her light, floral perfume.

Was she unattached? he wondered. Someone at the party—probably Mrs. Kelly, the busybody—had said the sisters were single, but that didn't mean Nicole didn't have a boyfriend.

She pointed out the circuit breaker. The landlord had taken the time to label them, and he turned off the breaker for the dining room.

"Can I see the new fixture?" he asked as they returned to the first floor.

Nicole showed him the box with the new, sleek light fixture. It was a popular model that he'd actually installed last week in a friend's house. Taking it out of the box, he held it, testing the weight. It was lighter than the old fixture.

Jeremy proceeded to take down the old chandelier as Nicole silently watched. Some of the wires were old and frayed.

"Good thing you're replacing this," he told Nicole. "The old one isn't looking too great. You don't want an electrical fire."

"We didn't like the way it looked, and our dad thought it should be replaced, so we took his advice," she remarked.

"He was right." Jeremy examined the box in the ceiling. It would have no trouble handling the new, lighter fixture. "Your landlord should have replaced this long ago."

Nicole stayed in the background, not interrupting him, while he installed the new fixture.

"There." He stepped away. "This was pretty easy."

"Not to me, it wouldn't be." Nicole was smiling when he glanced at her. "I don't know anything about electricity except that it can be dangerous."

He grinned. "That's a start."

"Do you want that soda now? I have colas or root beer," she said.

"Sure, a Coke would be fine."

She went into the kitchen, and he heard her sister on the stairs.

Marla was holding a purse, and a uniform was draped over her arm. "It's great to know an electrician," she said, smiling too. "We may have to call you again."

"Call any time." He meant it.

"Just curious—you have one of the largest homes on the block. Do you live there alone?" she asked abruptly.

"Yes," he answered. Was she trying to find out if he was single? He couldn't help grinning. Both sisters were beautiful, though Nicole had a friendlier smile.

Nicole had returned, a can of soda in her hand. She stared at her sister.

"Oh, we, ah, thought we saw someone else coming out of there the other day," Marla said hastily. "Maybe I was mistaken."

"That was probably my sister, Brooke," Jeremy said, amused. So they *were* trying to figure out if he was single!

"She comes over and hangs out with me about once a week. Her washing machine broke and her new one won't be delivered until today, so she's been doing laundry at my place. Is she short and blond?"

Both sisters nodded.

"That's her. She lives only fifteen minutes from here, in Hackettstown."

Marla looked at her watch. "Oh, I have to go! I have a couple of errands to do before work." She glanced at Nicole, smiling. Jeremy couldn't help seeing the annoyed look Nicole sent her sister in return. "Nice to meet you! Nicole will pay you." And Marla dashed out of the house.

Slowly, Nicole extended the hand that held the soda. "Sorry about that. My younger sister is a little nosy."

"It's no problem." Jeremy popped the top on the cola and took a long, refreshing gulp.

"We also have homemade brownies. Do you want some?" Nicole asked.

Would he like some homemade brownies? "Yes!" he practically yelled.

She smiled and disappeared, reappearing a few seconds later with a platter loaded down with chocolate brownies with glossy icing. "I made them a little while ago. I love to cook and bake, and Marla made the icing—she likes baking and cake decorating."

He took one, sat on the beige couch, and bit into it. *Ohh, he'd died and gone to heaven.*

"Wow, this is great." He closed his eyes, chewing, savoring the sweet, fudgey treat—delicious! He opened his eyes, finished it, and grabbed for another one. A part of his mind scolded him—he was acting like a savage, scarfing down these brownies like a starving man. "These are awesome—the best. You have a real talent."

Nicole was smiling at him. As she stood there, he was struck again by how pretty she was. If he wasn't so busy eating, he'd want to run his fingers through her hair—which was just as glossy as the icing.

"Take as many as you want," she offered.

He reached over and plucked a third one. She joined him on the couch, placing the platter on the old wooden coffee table, and bit into hers more delicately.

"I could make a meal of these." He swallowed, the dense sweetness unbelievably satisfying.

Her smile widened. "That wouldn't be too nutritious."

"I guess not." Wow, a woman who could bake brownies like these was someone special. "Hey, I was planning to go out on my boat this afternoon. Want to join me?"

He saw regret on her face. "Oh, I'd love to, but I'm going to a baby shower this afternoon for one of the girls at work. Can I have a rain check?"

"Sure." He eyed the platter, contemplating taking a fourth brownie. "Where do you work?"

"I'm an English teacher at Green Valley Middle School," she told him. "I teach seventh-grade students. I've also taught a cooking class in their adult school."

"Baking?" he guessed. "Do you need anyone to taste test?"

She laughed, and the sound was sparkling, pleasing, as delicious as the brownies. "It was a class in Italian cooking—and, as far as being a taste-tester goes, well . . . I do have a favor to ask."

Nicole regarded Jeremy. She'd been struck immediately by how good-looking he was. He was tall—over six feet—with midnight-black hair and olive-toned skin, and absolutely gorgeous green eyes. He was slim and had classic features—a nice nose and a mouth that turned up into an inviting smile, showing white teeth. But most of all, he seemed like a nice, down-to-earth guy. She guessed he was around her age.

She'd watched him work on the dining room light fixture. He moved methodically, removing the old fixture, then hanging the new one. As he worked she couldn't help noticing his wide, masculine shoulders and strongly defined muscles. Did he work out? she wondered.

She wondered, too, about asking him to appear on her show. Marla had managed—in a blatantly obvious way—to ascertain that Jeremy probably didn't have a girlfriend. Should she ask him about her show?

Why not? part of her brain had argued.

As she watched him, she waffled on her decision in her head. She hardly knew the man. But he definitely looked like a boyfriend she'd want to have by her side.

Then he'd gobbled up the brownies. She couldn't have asked for a more serendipitous sign that he was a good one to approach than when he'd said he wanted to taste test her cooking!

He was a typical bachelor anxious for a home-cooked meal—a meal made by her.

She swallowed.

"What favor?" Jeremy was asking. She saw him eyeing the platter of brownies. He'd eaten three already. He must have been starved.

"I, well, I was asked months ago to do a cooking show on the local cable network," she told him. Quickly, before she lost her nerve, she filled him in on her show, *A Taste of Romance.* He was listening carefully, focused on her words. As he leaned closer, she caught a faint whiff of a woodsy aftershave.

"A few months ago my producer asked me to mention a boyfriend," Nicole continued, "even though I don't have one."

"You don't?" He sounded surprised.

"No, not right now I don't. You don't have a girlfriend, do you?" she asked.

He shook his head, and a curious expression appeared on his face.

"Last night, after we taped an episode, Irene—my producer—took me aside." Nicole's words slowed and she hesitated. "She said that Thomas Clarkson, our executive producer, wanted to increase the male audience for the show. He thought the best way to do that was for my 'boyfriend' to appear on some episodes." She felt peculiar, asking a guy she hardly knew to play the part of a devoted boyfriend. That must be why her heart was beating rapidly.

Now she paused again and regarded Jeremy warily. He was calmly listening, his position relaxed.

"He wants the audience to see a boyfriend who doesn't exist," he said.

"Yes. So now"—the words stuck somewhere in her throat—"now I have to come up with a boyfriend for the show. I did suggest to Irene that I pretend I just broke up with the boyfriend, but she said Thomas really wanted him to appear because he was sure it would help improve ratings. My show airs twice a month, and also repeats, and they have two other cooking shows, but . . . they felt mine had the best potential to attract new male viewers."

She paused again, uncomfortable under Jeremy's quiet scrutiny. Flustered, she decided the best way to ask was simply to get it out. She rushed on. "So . . . would you consider playing the part of my boyfriend?"

Jeremy leaned forward, and Nicole saw a sudden gleam in those remarkable green eyes.

"That depends," he drawled. He gave her a wicked grin. "I'll do it if you can let me sample one of those meals every week. Can you cook for me?"

Jeremy watched Nicole's eyes widen in response to his words.

"You want me to cook for you?" she gasped.

"Yeah, as in a homemade meal." He grinned at her. "Consider it a payment for services rendered."

"Oh! Ah, sure," she said hastily. "I'll be glad to. What kind of foods do you like to eat?"

"Anything Italian is fine with me." If her brownies were this good, he could imagine what other delicious stuff she'd cook up.

"My grandmother's lasagna is one of my favorites," she said. "I'm cooking that on the next episode."

"That would be great," he said.

"I'll make garlic bread and a salad to go with it, just like I'm going to do on the show," she added.

A complete, home-cooked meal. "Great!" He knew he sounded like an eager kid, but he didn't try to curtail his enthusiasm.

She smiled suddenly. "I guess you don't cook too much for yourself?"

He shook his head. "I never really learned." Thinking about his home and the housekeepers who did most of the cooking—which was often bland—he added, "My mom's not much of a cook. I can boil water for pasta and slap on some store-bought sauce"—was Nicole actually shuddering at his words?—"and grill hot dogs and burgers, but that's about it."

"Well, I don't mean to brag, but I think you'll like my Grandma Rosa's lasagna a lot."

"I'm sure I will." He was practically salivating already. "I'm getting the better end of the bargain, believe me."

She tilted her head. "Do you think so?"

Chapter Three

Nicole studied the dining room table she'd carefully set with her red tablecloth and napkins. Her serviceable cutlery and simple dishes weren't anything much to look at, but the crystal goblets for wine and water that she'd bought at a yard sale added an elegant touch.

Should she add candles? she wondered for the hundredth time. She did on her show, but this was a dinner for a friend. Actually, it was kind of a rehearsal—not really a romantic dinner like the ones she arranged on TV.

"Use the candles," Marla said, coming down the stairs.

Nicole whirled around. They'd had this discussion only an hour earlier. Marla was obviously in favor of cultivating a romantic atmosphere.

"Yes," Marla continued, joining Nicole by the table. "Why not have a romantic dinner like on your show? He's cute and he's available. Make the most of it!"

She'd said the same thing already. "I'm still thinking about it," Nicole said. Then she changed the subject. "You look nice."

Marla was going out tonight with Dan, a nurse at her hospital. He was one of many guys who asked Marla out, but she was pretty selective. Like Nicole, she had once suffered a broken heart, and Nicole knew her sister was content to keep things casual with the guys she dated. This was only the second time she'd been out with Dan.

"Thanks. We're going out to that new Japanese place."

"Let me know how their food is," Nicole said as the doorbell rang.

Marla let Dan in, and they all spoke briefly. They departed, and Nicole was left to regard the table again.

She was tempted to put the nice crystal candlesticks on the table. Would Jeremy think that was silly? This dinner wasn't a date, exactly—just part of a bargain.

For one moment, she realized she wished it *was* a date.

Don't be ridiculous, she told herself.

She glanced at her watch. It was Friday evening, six-thirty, and Jeremy was due here in half an hour. The lasagna was bubbling in the oven, the salad and dessert were made and sitting in the refrig, and she had the garlic bread ready to pop in the oven in a few minutes. She had a few moments now to dash upstairs to her room, check her makeup, and comb her hair. She'd already changed from the nice pants and shirt she'd worn for teaching today to a denim skirt and cream-colored top.

Once she was ready, she walked slowly down the stairs. The table did look bare. Impulsively she went to the cabinet and took out her candlesticks and white candles.

She had just put the garlic bread in the oven when the doorbell rang.

He was early.

When Nicole opened the door, a warm sensation flowed

through her. She'd been thinking about Jeremy on and off all week, but up close his handsome face was even more compelling than in her mind. He was dressed in khakis and a short-sleeved light blue shirt. His dark hair, which he wore on the longish side, was neatly combed. His eyes were as green as she remembered.

"Hi," he said eagerly, and thrust out a bouquet of flowers.

"Oh, how sweet! You didn't have to do that," Nicole said, a part of her melting inside. "Thank you!" She sniffed at the flowers, a collection of daisies and mums and red carnations.

Jeremy entered the house, sniffing. "Mmm—I can't wait to eat!"

Of course—he was here for the food, not for her company.

Still, he didn't have to bring flowers. She felt touched. "I'll get a vase," Nicole said hastily, shutting the door.

Jeremy followed her into the dining room, and she rooted through the cabinet to take out her favorite vase. Walking into the kitchen, she filled it with water and placed the flowers carefully inside.

"Where did you learn to cook?" Jeremy asked from behind her.

She turned to him. "My mom is a pretty good cook, but my Grandma Rosa—her mother—is the real expert in our family. I used to love watching her, and she often let me help. She did a lot of cooking without using recipes, but I've written down most of them."

"Is she still alive?" Jeremy asked, glancing around the kitchen.

"Yes, she's still alive, but she's slowed down since my grandfather died three years ago, and she doesn't cook all the big meals she used to." Nicole sighed. At least she still had her grandmother, even though she was getting older.

"You're lucky. My father's parents died many years ago, and my mother's parents live in Florida now," Jeremy said. "This kitchen is a nice size," he added.

It was, which was one of the things Nicole really loved about the house. She had plenty of room to experiment with her cooking. The cabinets were old and the floor a cheap vinyl, but the appliances were new.

Nicole knew she and Marla were lucky they'd found the rental through a friend of hers at work. Near the lake in Mt. Olive, it wasn't large—a living room, dining room and kitchen; one and a half baths, and two good-sized bedrooms, plus a basement—but it suited them perfectly. It was only about half an hour away from their parents and an hour or so from where their brother went to college. Both sisters only had fifteen- to twenty-minute rides to work, so the location was ideal.

"I love this kitchen," Nicole said. "And I'm sorry about your grandparents and that you don't get to see your other grandparents much. They do add so much to our lives, don't they? My father's parents are gone now too." She moved back to the dining room and placed the flowers at one end of the table so they wouldn't block the view of each other when they sat down to eat. "Let me just check on dinner. It should be ready soon."

Jeremy followed her back to the kitchen, and she wondered if he was hungry or just really interested in the food—or maybe a little of both.

"You can take the salad out of the fridge," she suggested as she bent to open the oven door.

The lasagna and garlic bread were almost ready. When she straightened and closed the door, peeling off her oven mitts, Jeremy had placed the salad on the kitchen counter and was staring at her.

"That smells wonderful." His expression was eager, his eyes glowing.

Her grandmother's favorite saying flashed through Nicole's head: *The way to a man's heart is through his stomach.*

"Is that why Grandpa wanted to marry you?" Nicole had innocently asked when she was a child.

Her grandmother always smiled. "It was part of it, *cara mia.*"

Nicole stared at Jeremy now as two conflicting emotions pulled her in opposite directions.

Jeremy seemed like a nice guy, friendly and upbeat, not to mention handsome—very handsome. She'd like to get to know him better.

On the other hand, she wasn't sure if she was ready for anything more than an occasional meal and surface relationship with any guy. And this *was* a business arrangement. Maybe the best thing for her was just that.

"Nicole?"

With a start she realized he had asked something. "Sorry, I was daydreaming for a minute. What did you say?"

He crossed his arms. "Hope those daydreams were about me," he teased.

She flushed, but refused to answer.

"I asked if there's anything else you'd like me to do?"

She took the salad bowl and handed it to him. "You can put this on the dining room table. I'll get the salad dressing. And then you can pour the wine."

Within a few minutes they were seated at the table, starting on the salad, garlic bread, and red wine. The candles glowed softly, lending an intimate feel to their dinner.

"Gosh, even the salad is good," Jeremy said, picking up another forkful of lettuce and chopped fresh vegetables. She was amused to see how enthusiastically he attacked the food.

A moment later he picked up a piece of the aromatic bread. "This is delicious too—extraordinary. And we haven't started on the main course yet."

Nicole chewed thoughtfully, enjoying the momentary glory and satisfaction of creating an appealing meal.

She asked him about his job and if he'd always wanted to be an electrician.

"No," he answered, taking a second piece of garlic bread. "I studied business in college. I kind of thought I might be an accountant like my older brother, or go into the corporate world. I tried both after graduating, but was bored. I'd always liked working with my hands—I used to build stuff and wire things to move, like a windmill set I put together one time as a kid—and I finally made the decision to apprentice as an electrician a few years ago. So, here I am with my own business. The business degree did help in learning how to run my own company," he finished, and bit into the crusty bread.

"Well, good for you for following your dreams," Nicole said, taking a piece of bread for herself. "Did your parents object?"

"Nah, they pretty much felt we should all follow our dreams. There's four of us—Rebecca, Troy, Brooke, and me. Rebecca did follow in our dad's footsteps, and she became a doctor."

"What kind?" asked Nicole, curious. She reached for her wineglass.

"She's in orthopedics."

"And Brooke—she's the sister who lives in Hacketts-town?"

"Yeah, she does stage scenery and design for Quemby College, and she teaches a couple of classes there on the history of theater." Abruptly, he changed the subject. "What about you?"

"My family doesn't sound quite as interesting as yours," Nicole admitted. "My dad and his brother own a printing business that used to be my grandfather's. My mom was home when we were little, but now she teaches preschool. Marla's a nurse in the preemie unit at the hospital, and Joey's studying business at Rutgers."

"And how'd you get into teaching and cooking on TV?"

"I always loved reading and the way languages work," Nicole said, sipping some of the mellow wine. "I did study Spanish and Italian, but decided to become an English teacher. And I always liked to cook. I thought of being a caterer, but didn't think I wanted to do it full time. But then my friend Doris—she's a guidance counselor at our school and her husband is the head of our adult school—said they were looking for someone to teach this Italian cooking class. It was a popular class in the community school, and the teacher was moving out of state. So I started doing that."

"And how'd you get on TV?" he asked, reaching for another piece of garlic bread. He crunched on it as she answered.

"Irene Abrams, one of the producers at the local cable TV channel, took my class last year. When they decided to do a couple of cooking shows, she approached me to do the romantic-dinners one. I jumped at it," she finished.

"Romantic dinners, huh?" he asked, raising his eyebrows, the teasing note back in his voice.

Nicole flushed. "Yes. I think I'll bring in the lasagna now," she said, and escaped to the kitchen.

Jeremy decided he should give some serious thought to hiring Nicole to cook for him every night. Or perhaps he should kidnap her and keep her in the kitchen.

The lasagna was the best he'd ever tasted. The meat sauce—that was wonderful, spicy and delicious. The cheese was creamy and tasty too. The noodles were not too soft, not too hard, just right. The whole combination would have him smacking his lips for days.

"This is the best," he said, for probably about the fourth time.

Nicole looked amused. "I'm glad you like it. This is what I'll be making on my show—the one that's taping next Friday. The one you're going to be on."

She'd already filled him in on what he had to do. She'd be demonstrating how to cook the meal and he'd come in at the end, sample it, and say a couple of complimentary things.

"I can't wait to tell the audience how good this is." He regarded her. "Seriously, Nicole, I've eaten in some great Italian restaurants, and this is the best lasagna I've ever had, hands down."

"Thanks." She flushed, looking prettier than ever.

She was dressed in a short denim skirt and white feminine top that showed off her gorgeous dark hair and rose-colored lips. She looked as good as the food on the table.

He reached for one more piece of lasagna.

"I just realized something," she said.

"What's that?" he asked, savoring the tasty dish.

"I don't even know your last name! When we called you about the light fixture, we just called the name on your truck. I like your company name, by the way—Lightning Fast. It's catchy."

"Brooke thought of the name." He chewed slowly, wanting to make the dinner last. He couldn't remember when he'd eaten a dinner that was this good.

"I'll have to introduce you on my show. So . . . what's your last name?"

"Perez." He added cautiously, "My dad's from Mexico," and then waited to see if she recognized the name further, feeling his muscles tense.

Apparently the name didn't mean anything extraordinary to her. "Jeremy Perez," she said slowly, rolling it around as if it were a tasty treat. "That sounds nice."

She gave no sign that she'd ever heard of Dr. Antonio Perez, the well-known New York orthopedic doctor, or heard of his wife, the even-better-known Sharon Maloney-Perez.

"Do you speak Spanish?" She sounded simply curious.

"Yeah, but I don't speak it that well." He grinned. "My father came here as a boy, so even he doesn't speak it that much."

"Where did you grow up, Jeremy?" she asked, picking up her goblet and taking another sip of wine.

"I was raised in Short Hills." He tensed again, wondering what her reaction to that would be. Most people in northern New Jersey knew that the Short Hills section of Millburn was a very wealthy area.

"I know where that is. I have cousins in West Orange, right nearby."

He was relieved when she asked him if he wanted to

wait a few minutes before having dessert. He was starting to feel full, and wanted to enjoy the dessert on its own.

He was feeling relieved, as well, that Nicole didn't act all impressed and go ga-ga over the fact that he was from a wealthy town. Unfortunately, a lot of women had been more interested in him after they learned where he came from and about his background—especially Monica.

He was *not* going to think about Monica. Especially not when he was here with a gorgeous woman who was friendlier than his old girlfriend—a woman who could cook like a gourmet chef.

"This meal," he said with an appreciative sigh, "was fantastic."

She smiled again and stood. "I'll clear, and we can have dessert in a little while."

He stood up too. "I'll help," he said.

His mother hadn't been much of a cook, and they'd certainly had enough household help, but she had drilled her kids into helping clean up after a meal.

"Thanks," Nicole said.

It didn't take long for them to clear the table. He helped stack the dishwasher as she put away the leftovers. "You can take some of the lasagna home if you want," she offered as she covered the casserole with aluminum foil.

He took a deep breath, inhaling the spicy scents of dinner. It smelled super. Someone should bottle the aroma. "That would be great."

They went into the living room and he sat on the comfy beige sofa.

"What kind of music do you like?" asked Nicole, rummaging through some CDs.

"Rock and roll, jazz, and Broadway tunes all sound good to me," he answered.

She put a CD in the player and sat beside him. He recognized the Beatles a moment later.

The music was bright and mellow and swirled smoothly through the room. The lights were low, and in the dining room nearby, the candles flickered.

For a few seconds they were silent. He wanted to do something to thank her, to let her know how much he appreciated the wonderful meal.

Before he could say anything, she said, "Next Friday, I'll have to bring the food in various stages for the different segments of the show. But afterwards, you can eat it again!"

"I'm looking forward to it already."

"While we're taping, you'll be watching most of the time," Nicole said. "At the end, when I set the table and put the food out, you'll join me. We'll taste a little and they want you to comment on the food."

"That will be *no* problem at all," Jeremy said. "Listen, this dinner was so great, and I've enjoyed being here." He had, he realized. He hadn't had such a good time in ages. "Do you want to use that rain check and come on the boat with me tomorrow?"

"I'd love to," she answered promptly. Her face lit up and the smile that curved her lips was contagious. He found himself smiling back—and scooting closer to her on the couch. "We can go out on the lake. Do you fish?" he asked.

"No," she said.

"Do you want to learn?" He saw her visibly hesitate, and laughed. "It's okay if you don't want to," he said. "We can just enjoy the water."

"That sounds good to me," she said, leaning back against the cushions.

For a moment they were silent, gazing at each other.

As he looked at Nicole's face, he forgot about her outstanding cooking. All he could think of was how beautiful she looked in the dim light, how warm, and friendly, and down-to-earth she was. Without thinking, he reached out and ran his fingers through her hair. The dark waves were like satin. He let his fingers slip through the strands, gazing at her large, beautiful brown eyes.

Close by, he heard the front door open. And then Nicole was pulling away as cool night air swept through the living room.

"I'm back, and Dan's with me," he heard someone say.

He looked up. Nicole was flushing as her sister and a red-haired man walked into the living room.

Marla eyed them both, and he was pretty sure she knew she had interrupted a nice cozy interlude.

"We were—we were just about to have dessert," Nicole said, jumping up. "Would you like to join us?"

"So you're going on his boat tomorrow afternoon?" Marla asked eagerly as she followed Nicole up the stairs.

They'd had dessert and coffee with Jeremy and Dan, and the guys had helped clean up before leaving. Jeremy had given Nicole a swift hug before leaving and said, "I'll see you around two tomorrow?"

Nicole paused and glanced back at her sister, who was smiling. "Yes."

The dishwasher hummed, and Marla spoke louder than usual. "I like him—Jeremy, I mean."

"So do I," Nicole said, sighing.

"So, that's good!" Marla responded brightly.

"Maybe," Nicole said slowly. She proceeded into her

room, which she'd painted a soft green the previous Sunday. She plopped down on her bed, and Marla sat beside her. "Maybe not."

"Well, he seems like a really nice guy, very sincere," Marla said.

"Yes, he's pretty friendly, and he practically waxed poetic about my cooking. I hope that's not all it is," Nicole said, frowning suddenly. "You know Grandma Rosa always says the way to a man's heart—"

"—is through his stomach," Marla finished. "I know. But he must like more than your food, Nic. When we entered the house it looked like we were interrupting something *very* interesting."

Nicole flushed. "Oh, he was just playing with my hair," she said lightly. "What about you? How'd you like Dan?"

"He's nice," Marla said nonchalantly. "But . . . I don't know . . ."

They were silent for a moment, and then Marla yawned. "I'm tired. I'm going to sleep," she said, and hopped off the bed.

"G'night," Nicole said.

After her sister departed, she sat for a moment. She *did* like Jeremy. He seemed to be easygoing and thoughtful, from what she could see.

But she'd thought Brad was nice and thoughtful too. And she'd been wrong. Very wrong.

Brad had liked her . . . mostly for her looks—and the fact that she was pleasant to be around.

She hoped Jeremy didn't like her just for her looks and for her cooking talents.

Chapter Four

Nicole was almost ready to go on the boat when she heard Jeremy's knock on the door.

She ran the brush through her hair one more time and then almost skipped down the stairs. She'd been looking forward to this afternoon since she'd opened her eyes this morning.

She swung open the front door. Jeremy stood there, a big smile on his face. She caught her breath. He was the poster of tall, dark, and handsome.

He wore jeans with a hole in one knee, a gray T-shirt that said *Electricians Have the Power to Shock You*, and old sneakers. Despite his worn clothes, he looked like a pop star.

"Come on in," she greeted him, smiling. "I'll be ready in a minute."

Her experience with boats was limited, but she knew that out on the water it could get windy and cool even though the day was warm. She'd worn jeans and a favorite red T-shirt, and had a gray sweatshirt with her in case she needed it.

"I had the leftover lasagna for lunch," Jeremy announced. "Boy, was that good!"

"Thanks," she responded. "I made some cookies to bring along." She saw his eyes widen, and he gave her a dazzling smile.

"Homemade cookies?" He made smacking sounds, and said, "Mm-mm."

"They're actually my mother's recipe, not my grandmother's," she said. She walked to the kitchen and took out the small, pretty basket she'd layered with napkins and the cream cheese cookies. "Should I bring some soda?"

"I have some on the boat," he told her.

As she picked up her sweatshirt, he nodded approvingly. "Good, it could get cool out there. I always keep a sweatshirt on the boat."

Nicole locked her door and placed her keys inside her purse, then slung it over her shoulder. Jeremy took the basket of cookies and peeked inside.

"I'll try not to steal any now and save them for later," he said with a chuckle. Taking her hand, he led the way.

The lake was only two blocks away, a straight walk down their street. Clouds moved across the sky as they walked. Nicole glanced up. "Looks like we'll have rain later."

"Yeah, we're supposed to get some," he said.

She liked walking with her hand in his larger one. His hand was warm and strong, and hers fit neatly inside his grasp.

"How long have you lived here?" she asked.

"About a year and a half," he answered. "One of my college friends came from Mount Olive, and I always liked it here. The house needed a lot of work when I bought it, and I got a good deal. I've been fixing it up, and it's almost finished. I have buddies who are plumbers and carpenters and roofers, so they've helped."

Jeremy's house was one of the largest homes on the block. "It's a very attractive house, and big," she said.

"I like having the space around me," he admitted. "I have room if my family or friends come to visit, and like I said, I got a good deal on it. I'd like to get a couple of dogs soon. I could even bring them with me in the van when I'm working so they wouldn't be alone every day," he added.

"That sounds good! I love dogs too," Nicole told him. "We always had dogs growing up. If Marla and I didn't work such long hours, we'd have one now. My parents have a big mixed-breed dog, and at least we get to see her often."

They reached the end of the street and climbed down the grassy slope to the dock. Jeremy pointed to his boat, a medium-sized, bright white motorboat. It bobbed up and down as Jeremy helped her in.

"This is really nice," Nicole said as she shifted her balance. "Where did you learn to operate a boat?"

For just a moment, he appeared to hesitate. Then he said, "Oh, my dad always liked boats. Sometimes we used to go out on one with friends down at the shore. I took lessons one summer when I was in college. I think that's one reason I really wanted to live here, to be near the lake, and have the opportunity to go out on a boat all the time."

With a few swift movements he cast off, and then they were out on the lake. He sat near her, steering the boat. "You can try steering later."

"I'd like that," she said, enjoying the brisk wind and refreshing air.

Jeremy's parents must be well-to-do if they sometimes went out on boats, Nicole surmised. And he'd grown up in Short Hills—part of Millburn. It was a very wealthy town—maybe the wealthiest—in New Jersey.

Yet Jeremy seemed remarkably down-to-earth—maybe one of the most down-to-earth people she'd ever met . . . unlike Brad.

But she didn't want to think about Brad and his snobby attitude—not on this pleasant afternoon! Firmly, she pushed her ex-boyfriend out of her mind.

Jeremy pointed out some landmarks, like the spot on the beach across the lake where a famous nightclub used to stand. "Jackie Gleason got his start there," he told her. "Later it became the town hall until they built the new one. Unfortunately, it was falling apart and they had to tear it down a few years ago."

"That's too bad," she said. "Jackie Gleason played there, huh? Wow, I didn't know we had anyone so famous here."

"It was a long time ago," he added hastily. "And over there is the Castle Theater where they do productions, including Shakespeare, during the school year for students from all over the state."

She knew of that. "Our high school always goes to see *Hamlet* every spring. And . . . what's that?" she asked, pointing.

"That's protected land, part of the state's Green Acres projects," he told her, steering out into the middle of the lake.

After a while he let the boat drift near a marshy shore, and they ate some of their cookies and drank soda. Watching him scarf down what must have been his sixth or seventh cookie, Nicole asked, "I guess you don't get home-baked cookies very often?"

"No-oo," he said, the word coming out like a groan. "Even at Christmastime, most of the cookies in my house came from the bakery."

"I'll bake you some," she said lightly. And then a picture flashed into her mind: sitting in front of a Christmas tree with Jeremy, handing him a dish piled high with frosted trees and snowmen.

She hoped she got the opportunity to bake cookies for him during the holidays! It was three months away, but she already knew she'd like to keep seeing him.

But was that wise? She couldn't answer that question, and didn't want to mentally debate it now.

He asked her about her classes, and she described the unit on mythology they were going to start the next week. Jeremy asked some more questions, and she got the impression that he was well-read.

"Where did you go to college?" she asked, curious.

"I graduated from Amherst. What about you?"

"I went to Rutgers. I was in a five-year program where I got my BA and MA together in teaching. My brother is at Rutgers now."

They spoke a little about their college classes, New Jersey football teams, and friends. Then Jeremy invited her to try steering the boat.

It was fun, and surprising. Nicole turned the wheel, but it took the boat longer to turn than a car, and she overcompensated. They were soon laughing at her amateurish attempts to steer.

After a little while, Jeremy took the wheel back and they glided over the lake, waving to a few other boaters who were out.

Mist flew into their faces, but Nicole didn't care. She was having fun, and she knew it wasn't just being out on a boat that was making her smile. It was being in Jeremy's company.

It didn't seem much time had passed at all when Jeremy said suddenly, "I think it's going to rain soon."

She looked upwards, and sure enough, storm clouds now encompassed the sky.

"I don't want us to get caught in a thunderstorm," he added. "Guess we better head back to shore."

They docked the boat, and Nicole helped him gather up their things as a low rumble of thunder reached them. Light rain began to hit her face.

Jeremy reached for her hand, and together they walked back to their homes.

"That was fun!" she declared, genuinely sorry to see the afternoon end.

"And those cookies were delicious," he said, his eyes gleaming. "Hey, why don't you come over to my place for dinner and we'll watch a movie or something?"

Nicole raised her eyebrows. "You're cooking?" She tried to keep from sounding astonished.

He grinned. "I was thinking of ordering pizza—that is, if you like pizza."

"I love it," she said.

They decided to go to a nearby video place and each select a movie. "Brooke and I like to collect movies," he told her. "I'll buy two—you pick one and I'll pick the other."

It didn't take long to get to the video place in Jeremy's sporty-looking dark Jeep.

"I guess you use the van just for business?" Nicole asked. With high insurance rates in New Jersey, she was surprised to see he owned more than one vehicle.

"Yeah, on weekends I like to drive this," he acknowledged.

Once at the crowded video place, they separated to pick out movies. Nicole wasn't sure whether to select a romantic comedy she was sure she'd enjoy—Jeremy might think it was a "chick flick" and not enjoy it as much as she would. She looked around, spotting some classics on sale in one corner, and finally chose an old Agatha Christie mystery.

Jeremy appeared with a recent action-adventure movie, the kind that looked like it had buildings being blown up and car chases. It was typical guy fare, Nicole thought.

He saw the movie in her hand. "That's a good choice."

"You've seen this movie?" she asked, holding up *Murder on the Orient Express.*

"Years ago. My mom used to rent classic movies, and our family would watch them together."

"That's cool," Nicole murmured. His mom might not cook, but she sounded interesting. Before she could ask more, Jeremy had plucked the movie out of her hand. "Remember, it's my treat."

She thanked him, and they were soon on their way back. They stopped to pick up a pizza at Enzo's, debating lightly on toppings, and settling on half plain and half pepperoni.

Once back at Jeremy's, Nicole looked around.

His house was large, and she could see immediately that it had been updated. The living room and dining room they passed were light and bright, with simple, modern furniture. He led the way to the kitchen, and she stopped, audibly gasping.

It was her dream kitchen come to life! Despite the dark day, the kitchen was bright. Stainless steel appliances, a commercial stove, dark granite counters, and cherry cabinets—it looked like something from a home design show. A ceramic tile floor and glass tile backsplash completed the high-end look.

"This is gorgeous!" she exclaimed.

"I put in all top-of-the-line stuff when I remodeled," Jeremy said, setting down the pizza box on a simple round table near a sliding glass door. "My friends Ryan and Matt helped me. And Brooke helped me decorate. I guess it's a shame I don't cook."

"Any time you want lessons, just let me know," Nicole quipped, then stopped. She hadn't meant to say that. He might think she was being too pushy.

"Or maybe you'd like to cook your next meal for me here?" He raised his eyebrows. His voice *did* sound enthusiastic.

"It would be a pleasure," she said truthfully, glancing around. "You did a lot of work here. This is a dream kitchen."

"I'll give you the grand tour of my house after we eat," he promised.

He took out sodas, and she found paper plates and napkins in a cabinet. They were soon digging into the tasty pizza.

Nicole found herself relaxing as Jeremy talked about a few of the electrical jobs he'd finished during the last few weeks. He'd done everything from wiring a new, large addition on an existing home to upgrading the electric in a local house built during the 1940s.

In turn, she told him about some of her problem students, the ones who thought they didn't have to do homework or were too rebellious to want to do anything. "But the nice students make up for the bad ones," she finished.

Rain pinged against the windows and glass doors. The view of the spacious yard was pretty in the darkening evening. The rain had become a constant beat interspersed with low thunder and occasional flashes of lightning, but the sounds were soothing and comfortable.

When they finished the pizza, they left the last couple of slices in the large refrigerator and Jeremy gave her "the tour," as he called it.

Besides the living room, dining room, and kitchen, the downstairs featured a half bath, a laundry room, a family room with fireplace, and a sunroom that he said the previous homeowners had added to the existing house. Down in the finished basement he'd put in a pool table in one area. There was an additional TV with a couple of game consoles and a couch in another section, and a drum set in a corner.

"You play the drums?" Nicole asked.

"Yeah," he replied modestly.

"I play the French horn. Were you ever in a band?"

"In school, I was in the marching and concert bands."

"Yeah, I was too. Play something," she urged.

He sat down and in moments was playing loudly, coordinating the rhythm of the drums in something that sounded vaguely familiar.

She clapped her hands when he finished. "What was that from?"

He grinned. "It's part of Santana's 'Soul Sacrifice.' "

"It sounded wonderful!" she praised.

"How about a game of pool?" he suggested.

After playing two games of pool—which Nicole badly lost—Jeremy promised she could practice when she came over to cook next time.

"I'll show you the rest of the place," he offered.

So far, the house had been pleasantly if simply decorated, and the upstairs was much the same. They went up the stairs to a large room from which the other rooms opened up.

"This is kind of like my home office," Jeremy said, with a sweep of his hand. The room held two comfortable-looking armchairs, two desks—one with a computer and one with a laptop—and a couple of bookcases. A glance showed that Jeremy's preferred reading was mystery and suspense novels.

One of the desks was an old captain's desk with a pull-down cover. "That's a beautiful antique," Nicole remarked, stepping over to examine it.

"It belonged to my great-grandfather," Jeremy told her. "I always liked it, so my mother gave it to me."

She shot him a glance. Certainly if this desk was any indication, he must have grown up among valuable things. Yet he didn't show them off or act as if they were very important. He didn't act like he was impressed with himself—unlike Brad.

Once again she shoved her old flame from her mind.

On the captain's desk was a framed color photo. Nicole bent to study it. Jeremy stood beside another man who looked a lot like him, but was perhaps a little older, and his hair was a light shade of brown. Next to them were the short blond young woman she knew was his sister Brooke, and another woman who had dark auburn hair and was short too. Flanking them was an older, exotic-looking man with graying hair and a short, blond woman who looked a lot like Brooke—and very well preserved for the age she must be.

"That's Troy, Rebecca, Brooke, and me," he told her, "with our parents."

"What a good-looking family!" Nicole exclaimed.

He grinned. "It was taken a few years ago at my cousin's wedding. Here, I'll show you the rest of the rooms."

Nicole got to peek into two guest bedrooms, Jeremy's large master bedroom, two luxurious bathrooms, and an empty room he was using for storage, containing a table and a couple of boxes.

"Wow, you have a lot of space here," she said.

"Like I said, the house was a bargain," Jeremy said. "But I have used the guest rooms. A few weeks ago, Rebecca and her husband stayed over." He changed topics. "Well, let's go watch a movie!"

They watched the Agatha Christie mystery first. They both enjoyed it, and the acting was superb. After it ended, they finished the cookies and discussed the plot and acting. Nicole found Jeremy's observations to be interesting and thoughtful.

Outside the rain continued, but inside, on the couch in Jeremy's family room, the atmosphere was warm and cozy. Jeremy had gradually inched closer, and as they began watching the action adventure movie, he put his arm around Nicole's shoulder.

That felt right. Like she belonged in the circle of his arm, she thought.

The movie turned out to be suspenseful and more interesting than she'd originally thought it would be. When it was over he clicked off the DVD player and flipped through some channels.

"That was good," he remarked.

"Yes, it was," Nicole said. Before they could discuss the film, she noticed what was on the TV as he went from one channel to the next. "Oh, look! One of my favorite cooking shows is on!"

He paused and backtracked to it. The show on the big-screen TV was *Chef vs. Chef,* which she enjoyed watching immensely. Some of the episodes were on late during the week, so she didn't get to see it all the time. It was on at eleven on Saturday nights, and if she wasn't out with friends on weekends she liked to watch it.

"What is it?" asked Jeremy.

Nicole explained how two top chefs competed against each other, creating several dishes in the space of an hour. "Would you like to watch?" she asked, wondering if he'd agree.

"Sounds interesting," Jeremy said, and leaned back, once again placing his arm around her shoulders.

Instinctively Nicole cuddled into his embrace, and remained there as they watched the two chefs and their staffs creating their culinary masterpieces. Jeremy didn't seem bored—in fact, he looked interested.

"I guess your show isn't competitive like this," he remarked.

"No, it's just me," she said, as they observed one of the chefs whipping up a meringue for a pie.

They watched the hour-long show, with Jeremy asking questions about a couple of things. She explained why using real garlic gave a superior flavor to garlic powder and why chocolate had to be melted carefully. He actually seemed interested in her answers.

"I'm looking forward to your show next week," he said as the TV show ended.

"So am I," she agreed, realizing with a start that she was looking forward to the segment more than she usually did. And it was almost a week away!

He yawned. "Sorry, I was up early—I had to work this morning."

"That's okay. I'll get going," Nicole said. She'd had a fun time but didn't want to overstay her welcome.

The rain had slowed to a drizzle, but Jeremy insisted on

walking her home across the street, holding an umbrella over her head.

She saw the miniblinds in the house diagonally across the way move slightly. Nicole suppressed a grin and pretended she hadn't noticed. Vera Kelly, her elderly neighbor, was a doll, but very nosy. She knew everybody in the area and everything about the neighborhood. She would have noticed that Nicole was spending time with Jeremy and was probably watching to see how late she stayed at his house.

Nicole's house was dark—Marla was working a late shift tonight—and at the door she paused, fumbling for her keys.

"I had a great time today," she said sincerely.

"I did too." Jeremy leaned down and brushed her lips with his, just a soft kiss—yet every cell in her body seemed to warm like the sauces that simmered on the cooking show.

Almost without thinking, she placed her hands on his shoulders. Jeremy drew her close, and this time his lips pressed against hers, hard.

After a minute or two they parted. Nicole's head seemed to be skimming over waves just as the boat had today.

"Good night," he said, his voice dropping to a husky timbre. "I'll call you next week." He touched her face lightly.

"Good night," Nicole said, her voice faint. She unlocked her door, her hands not quite steady, and entered her home.

What a kiss! She felt as light as the meringue she'd seen on TV only a short while ago. Jeremy's kiss had been electrifying!

Nicole left one dim living room lamp on for Marla, then went upstairs.

Inside her bedroom, she moved to the window. Both bedrooms in the house they rented were the same size, but

Marla often worked late and slept in, so she wanted the room facing the quiet backyard. Nicole, who had to get up early for school, had the bedroom in the front.

She paused in the act of pulling down the shade. From her window she had a full view of Jeremy's house directly across the street. There was a light on somewhere upstairs, but as she watched, it was turned off. He'd probably gone straight to sleep.

She was still a little too keyed up for sleep, so she picked up the romance novel she'd started reading the other day, and climbed into bed.

Her thoughts, though, began to tumble together.

It seemed obvious that, coming from Short Hills and having a father who was a physician, Jeremy came from an upper-class family. And although he didn't seem like a status-conscious snob, she had been deceived once before— by Brad, who had fooled her badly.

She'd met Brad shortly after she'd graduated from college. He'd come from a rich family that lived in an upscale community in Bergen County. At first he had seemed sincere. She'd fallen for him, hard. And she admitted to herself that she'd liked it when he'd taken her to exclusive restaurants and gotten tickets to Broadway shows and to popular sporting events.

He'd seemed to like showing her off and talking about how beautiful she was. After a while, Nicole had begun to have some doubts. Brad had seemed so consumed by her looks, so eager to escort her around where they'd be seen, but she had pushed her misgivings to the back of her mind—which had been a mistake.

It wasn't until her cousin Kim, who was volunteering at a cancer charity fundraiser, had seen Brad with his arm around a tall blond that Nicole realized she should have trusted that little voice in her head.

She'd confronted him, and it had been ugly. At first Brad had denied he was seeing someone else. Then he'd finally admitted he had a "kind of" girlfriend, someone he'd known for years. Their families expected them to get engaged, but JoAnna—his girlfriend—had been running around with a couple of different guys. Brad's aim had been to make her jealous. Being seen with Nicole was accomplishing that.

He'd assured Nicole that he did care for her, but she'd been devastated. How could he string her along when he really wanted someone else? Heartbroken, she'd ended their relationship then and there. He'd continued to call her on and off for a couple of months, but she'd refused to see him.

The last she heard, Brad and JoAnna were officially engaged—but still seeing other people on the sly.

Nicole sighed now and closed her book, unable to concentrate on it. She wanted nothing to do with Brad's kind of mentality, with people who traveled in society circles but cheated on and used others for their own purposes.

She liked Jeremy—liked him a lot. But if he was anything like Brad, she would—well, she'd just have to see. Right now, he was simply a friend, doing her a huge favor. And she was grateful for that.

And, despite their kiss, it could very well be that a friend was all he would ever be.

Chapter Five

So when do I get to meet this cooking genius?" Brooke asked.

Jeremy straightened and looked at his sister. "You want to meet her?"

He was at Brooke's condo, looking over an old lamp she'd found at a thrift shop that she thought would be perfect for one of the scenes in the new play the college was doing. But the frayed electrical cord had alerted her to a potential problem.

"Yes, I would," she said. "Aside from her being a cooking wiz, I haven't heard you sound this excited about any woman in—well, in years."

Jeremy considered that. He'd definitely been excited when he first met Monica. Since that catastrophe, he couldn't think of anyone else he'd gotten really enthusiastic about.

"I guess you're right," he said slowly, "about that and about this too." He nodded toward the lamp, deliberately changing the topic. "It definitely needs rewiring. I can do it sometime this week if you want."

"That would be great," she said.

It was Tuesday evening, and as they often did on Tuesdays, they'd gotten together at a casual restaurant for dinner. Brooke had asked him to check the lamp she'd found, and they now stood in her work area, where she had scenery sketches, some props, and general arts and crafts stored in the family room in the finished basement.

He hoisted up the lamp, which appeared to be from the 1940s or even the '30s, and carried it back up to the main level. Brooke trailed after him.

"Sooo . . . ," she said as she returned to the subject of Nicole, "when can I meet her?"

"I'm not sure that's a good idea." Jeremy set the lamp down by Brooke's front door.

"Why not?" his sister demanded.

He sighed. Were all families this meddling, or just his? At twenty-nine he was the youngest sibling, and it seemed his brother and sisters thought they were entitled to know everything about his life. And that was not to mention what his parents thought!

Brooke reached out and tugged his arm. "Come on, let's sit and talk about this."

He let her lead him into the living room and over to her big comfy leather sectional. Once they were seated together, she asked him again, "Why don't you want her to meet me?"

"It's not just you. It's the whole family," he said.

Brooke raised her eyebrows. "What do you mean 'the whole family'? Why don't you? Oh, no," she said suddenly. The green eyes which were so like his own reflected comprehension. "You mean you're still not telling people—"

"That's right," Jeremy said. "I don't want them to know

our mother is Sharon Maloney-Perez and our dad is Doctor Antonio Perez."

Brooke stared at him with an accusing look in her eyes.

"You know it's not because I'm embarrassed or ashamed or anything," he began.

"No, it's because you're just frightened." She sighed, her expression softening. "I guess I can understand that, although I only had one guy who wanted to be my boyfriend because he thought it would get him in the door of the theater world."

"I've had several girlfriends who thought that," Jeremy said.

"There've been several?" Brooke asked. "I don't remember that."

"You should. You were only a year ahead of me in school. But then, you were all wrapped up in William." He had been Brooke's high school sweetheart. "Remember Cassandra, Brandi, and Chelsea? They all had acting aspirations and were sure that getting close to me—and to Mom— would help their future acting careers."

Brooke sighed. "I do remember Chelsea, although the other two are vague. Okay, so it happened, I guess especially since we sometimes appeared on *All My Relatives*."

"Yeah." Being occasional guests on the show in which their mom had starred for over thirty-five years meant that many people thought he and his brother and sisters would go into acting too. And a lot of people thought cozying up to him would be a good way to further their own show-business ambitions. "And in college, I had two girlfriends who it turned out were interested in me for the same reason. And then Monica came along . . ."

He stopped. Brooke, of all his siblings, was closest to him in age and temperament and understood how hurt he'd been by Monica three years ago. He'd fallen for Monica, and had even been contemplating marriage, when he'd overheard her one day on her phone. She'd been complaining to her friend that it was taking him so long to introduce her to his family, and she was so anxious to quit her administrative job and really get into her true calling— the theater.

As he'd listened, it had become obvious even from the one-sided conversation that Monica had planned this all along. She'd learned about his mother and their family; she'd deliberately sought him out at a charity function his family supported; she'd pretended to care for him, all the while wanting to use him to get friendly with his mother and get on the show.

The sad thing was, not only did he have no clue about this while it was happening; he hadn't even realized that Monica had acting experience and ambitions. He'd just been caught up in having a good time with her, and he'd thought she genuinely cared for him.

When she'd gotten off the phone, he'd put an abrupt end to their relationship.

He sighed now, regarding Brooke. Their mother, Sharon, was a famous actress; their father, Antonio, was famous because not only was he a well-respected doctor, but many people knew of their star-struck romance. The beautiful young actress who had broken a finger, been treated by the handsome Mexican doctor, had a whirlwind romance, and then had a marriage that had lasted over thirty-five years and was still going strong—it was one for the story-books . . . and the tabloids.

"So, no," Jeremy continued, "I'm not telling anyone. When I moved to Mount Olive, I decided to continue to hide our family background. Perez isn't an unusual name, and no one here has associated me with the famous Sharon Maloney-Perez and Doctor Antonio Perez. I'm not telling a soul! I even put all the family photos upstairs so no one sees them when they come into the house."

Brooke frowned. "But you're older and wiser now," she pointed out. "Don't you think that if someone was using you, you'd catch on pretty quickly?"

He shook his head. "No, I'm not taking that chance. I don't want anyone to know. Although I had a scare with Nicole. I was showing her the house, and I forgot about the family photo on my desk. Luckily, she didn't recognize Mom in that."

"Do you really think you can't trust her?" Brooke asked, leaning against the cushions.

"I'm not taking any chances," he stated.

"She might find out at some point," Brooke said.

"Unless someone tells her, I'll be safe," Jeremy said. "I want someone who likes me for myself alone, sis."

"I understand." Brooke reached out and gave him a sudden, fierce hug. "I certainly won't say anything." She pulled back and stared at him. "But she could find out eventually, bro, if you keep seeing her."

"I'll worry about that if and when it happens," he said.

When the door to the studio opened, Nicole anxiously looked up.

Jeremy entered the area.

She caught her breath. He'd been handsome before in his T-shirts and jeans, but in a black shirt with the cuffs rolled up, a black-and-white striped tie and black jeans, he looked more than handsome. He looked gorgeous—like a male model, or a Latino superstar.

He caught sight of her and gave his signature, casual grin.

She'd been nervous since she arrived at the studio. After months on the show, that was unusual for her, and she knew it was because of Jeremy.

She wasn't just anxious because the producers were hoping this segment would bring in more viewers. It was because she'd be interacting on camera with Jeremy, in close proximity to him, playing the part of a devoted girlfriend.

Could they pull it off?

She took a deep breath, approaching Jeremy. "Hi," she said, her voice low.

"Hi," he said, and leaning forward, planted a quick kiss on her lips. "Am I doing okay so far?" he asked, pulling back, his eyes gleaming.

"You look great," she said. She caught a whiff of his masculine, woodsy aftershave. She had an impulse to lean closer and kiss him back. Wow, he looked good . . . and he exuded a certain kind of masculine presence that the female viewers were going to love. At the same time, though, he just seemed like a down-to-earth guy—meaning that the whole TV audience would relate to him.

Nicole was sure relating to him. Her heartbeat had speeded up.

Their outfits would look good together, she thought. She had asked him if he had something black to complement the outfit she planned to wear. Nicole had dressed in a red, black, and white top with black pants that were comfortable and easy to move in.

She'd already set up the food, in various stages of being made, and had her utensils lined up on the studio's kitchen counter. She'd spent the last few minutes carefully setting up the china and crystal on the table where they would eat at the end of the show.

"I can't wait to sample the food again," Jeremy declared.

"Oh, there you are. This must be Jeremy," Irene said, rushing towards them. Her permed brown hair bounced around her round face.

Nicole introduced them, and after shaking hands, Irene said, "Can you come back here, Jeremy? We won't need you until the end. Allie will put a little makeup on you to give you more color. I hope you don't mind."

Nicole had never heard her producer so anxious to please. She must be feeling the pull of an attractive man— a very attractive man. She turned to look at Jeremy, wondering how a guy as masculine as he was would react to Irene's request.

He shrugged. "Okay."

She had to admire his cooperation. Some men would protest vehemently, she suspected.

Irene led Jeremy away, explaining that he could watch nearby until they taped the final segment.

Nicole checked her utensils and food again, and then Irene reappeared. "Okay, we're just about ready."

The show's music and logos would be edited in later. Nicole watched as Will and Ethan, the cameramen, finished with their equipment. Moments later, Will said, "We're all set."

Irene moved back, and Shelly, the director, took over. "Okay, let's rock and roll!" she said brightly.

Nicole welcomed her audience and spoke about today's menu. "Today I'm sharing my grandmother's secret lasagna recipe! Now, I've already made a simple salad . . ." She allowed time for one of the cameras to zoom in on the fresh salad resting in a handsome wooden bowl. "Any salad you like will do," she said. "We're going to keep that part easy, and focus on the lasagna and garlic bread. Ladies, your guys will love this! And let's be politically correct—for the guys who like to cook, your girlfriends will love this too. Everyone does."

She moved a chopping board and knife closer to where she was standing. "Now, for my special sauce, I'm going to chop up some onions and press fresh garlic." She demonstrated, then put the ingredients into a pan with some olive oil.

As Nicole cooked, she spoke about her grandmother and the ingredients, and showed the audience exactly what had to be done. She continually looked up and smiled. All the while she was conscious that Jeremy had come to sit in one of the seats behind the cameras, and was watching her.

"Now, while the meat sauce is simmering, we're going to make the cheese filling," she continued.

They took a couple of minutes' break while Shelly consulted with Irene on something. Will got a close-up of the simmering sauce.

Nicole moved towards Jeremy. "I hope you're enjoying the show," she said.

"I am," he assured her.

"You're a good sport about the makeup for the cameras," she added, hoping he wasn't embarrassed.

He shrugged. "It's no problem—although I'm wiping it off as soon as we get done." He reached out and lightly touched her hand. "Don't worry, I plan to play my part to perfection."

That should make her feel good, she thought after thanking him and going back to the kitchen set, but it worried her because she knew it would be so easy to imagine it wasn't a part he played—that he really was her boyfriend, sitting there, watching her cook, salivating over the tempting aromas.

She gave herself a silent shake.

When they went back to taping, Nicole moved over to a bowl and once again beamed at the audience.

"Now my grandmother's secret to getting the ricotta cheese really creamy is to add a couple of eggs," she told the audience. She added them, stirred, and continued, "I also like to add a little salt and pepper for extra flavor." The camera zoomed in as she worked.

"My boyfriend thinks my lasagna is the best he's ever tasted," she added, stirring the ingredients.

The next segments went well, with the exception of when a lasagna noodle went flying through the air. She could hear Jeremy's laugh. They retaped that part.

Finally they got to the segment where she finished setting the table and lit the red candles on it. Everything inside her tensed up. This was it.

"Everything's ready," she said, "and I think I hear Jeremy now!"

He responded right on cue, walking onstage with an assurance she admired. "Hey, sweetheart," he said breezily, and bent forward to give her a quick kiss on the cheek.

They'd gone over what he was to do the night before, and now he sat down in the seat opposite hers and flashed a smile at the camera. "Boy, does this smell great. I wish you could smell the aromas," he told the audience. He turned and grabbed a piece of garlic bread out of the basket she handed him. "I am one lucky guy."

Now *that* hadn't been part of their rehearsal session, but it seemed natural so she simply grinned in answer. Then, taking a piece of the finished lasagna she'd brought with her and merely reheated, she placed it on Jeremy's plate, letting Ethan get in for a close-up of the dish.

Ethan moved back and focused on Jeremy, who was chewing with a look of delight on his face.

"Wow, is this ever great!" He dug his fork in again. "This is the best lasagna I've ever eaten, hands down."

Ethan slowly backed away, so that the audience would see both Nicole and Jeremy in the final moments.

Nicole was smiling at the audience. "Remember, these recipes are on the station's Web site. Just look for *A Taste of Romance,* cook, and enjoy!" She made sure her smile was extra bright for the last few seconds.

"That's it!" Shelly exclaimed.

The cameras moved back, and Shelly added, "I don't think we'll have to do much editing on this one. That was a really good job, guys!"

Nicole looked at Jeremy, who was enthusiastically consuming the dish. "You can relax and eat, and we'll bring more home. I usually leave some for Will and Ethan."

"That sounds great. The show wasn't so hard," he said in a low voice, and winked at her.

"I'm going to have a word with Irene," Nicole told him.

Irene was already approaching when Nicole reached the counter. "Nicole, that was superb. The audience will love this. Jeremy's a natural, and the chemistry between you is so good!"

Startled, Nicole stared at her boss. "It is?"

"Of course—anyone can see the sparks flying between you two!"

They could? Nicole shot Jeremy a speculative look. He continued to eat, his attention riveted on his plate.

She was impressed by the fact that he hadn't been a nervous wreck, like so many people were in front of the TV cameras. Of course, this was taped, not live; but still, she'd observed other people in the studio become flustered and nervous. Jeremy just seemed to take it all in stride.

As she cleaned up, one by one the bright, hot lights were

shut down. A few minutes later Jeremy joined her and without asking, simply pitched in. It didn't take long for them to get the leftovers and half-made samples packed up.

"Did you enjoy the show?" Nicole asked, watching his expression in the semi-darkness of the studio. The cameramen and Irene had disappeared, and Shelly was off in a corner somewhere, jotting down notes.

"It was fun." He leaned closer. "I liked the food. And"—he stepped even closer and slid his hands around her waist—"even better, I liked the company." He gently tugged her closer.

She tilted her head up to gaze at him. Even in the dim light, his green eyes sparkled. Almost without thinking, she moved her hands and surrounded his waist, too, moving closer into his warm embrace. "I like the company too," she whispered.

And then his lips captured hers.

It was as if her whole being was sizzling like the lasagna she'd just cooked, bubbling over. Nicole felt the heat of the kiss down to her toes. As warmth suffused her, she kissed him back.

"Ahem." The half-cough, half-chuckle from nearby made Nicole step back. Jeremy still gripped her, but their faces pulled apart.

Shelly stood nearby, grinning. "I think we're done here and can shut off the rest of the lights. You lovebirds can take this outside."

Nicole felt herself flush and was about to protest when she remembered that Jeremy was supposed to be her boyfriend. They were supposed to act like lovebirds.

But that kiss hadn't been acting. She knew it in her bones.

That kiss had been the real thing.

Chapter Six

Jeremy glanced at Nicole. Her cheeks were a rose color. "Come on, I'll help you carry this stuff to your car," he suggested.

Nicole grabbed her jacket and Jeremy helped her put it on.

Silently, they carried the casseroles, the basket of bread, and the salad back to her car parked behind the studio. The early evening breeze was chilly.

But he was still warm. That kiss—wow—it had been electrifying, like he'd gotten a jolt from the strongest current!

Nicole opened her Chevrolet, and together they loaded her items into the back.

"Thanks again for doing this," Nicole said, shutting the door.

He'd had fun and didn't want the evening to end. Maybe they could spend more time together. "No problem. Hey, want to stop off for dessert somewhere? Not that I'm that hungry, but we could have coffee."

She agreed and suggested a café near their homes where they could get coffee or hot chocolate.

The weather had turned cooler during the last few days, with the crisp scents of autumn present in the late-September air. As a breeze gusted, Jeremy realized he'd left his jacket behind.

"I'll be out in a minute," he said to Nicole. "I left my jacket in the studio."

He entered the now almost-dark building and quickly found the lightweight windbreaker he'd thrown over a chair. He turned to find someone standing in front of him.

"Jeremy! I didn't have a chance to say hi before, but I recognized you as soon as you came in," said one of the cameramen.

Jeremy stared at the man. He was about Jeremy's age, tall, with blondish-brownish hair. He looked familiar, but for a moment Jeremy couldn't place him.

"Will Jenkins," the guy said, thrusting out his hand.

"Will—William? Hey!" Jeremy said, gripping his hand. It was William Jenkins, Brooke's devoted high school boyfriend. "How are you?"

As they shook hands, a peculiar feeling crept through Jeremy. William knew all about him, who he was, and about his family. William wouldn't say anything to Nicole, would he?

He bent towards William and said in a low voice, "It's good to see you. But, listen—Nicole doesn't know anything about my family. Don't give it away, okay?"

Surprise crossed William's face. "Okay . . . ," he drawled. He paused. "But if I do that, maybe you'll do a favor for me?"

"Sure," Jeremy said, then wondered if he should have

asked what the favor was first. But William had piqued his curiosity.

William took out his cell. "What's your number? I'll call you."

Jeremy rattled it off, watching Will. "So, what's the favor?" He said it casually as he shrugged into his jacket.

"Help me get in touch with your sister."

Jeremy stared at him, then started to laugh. "You want to get in touch with Brooke?" Relief wove through him.

"Yes," William said emphatically.

That should be easy enough, Jeremy thought. "That'll be no problem."

"There, that's done." Nicole surveyed the table in the dining room, complete with candles.

Tonight's dinner wasn't romantic—just a couple of friends coming over. But the candles did add a nice atmospheric touch.

Nicole returned to the kitchen to find Marla swirling her homemade chocolate-buttercream icing on the cupcakes.

"These are finished," Marla announced as she completed the last one.

"They look good," Nicole said.

It was Sunday, and the weekend was going by quickly. She and Jeremy had had hot chocolate and brownies together on Friday, and then they'd called it a night. He'd told her he was working part of Saturday and then going to a baseball game with a friend.

During Saturday morning, Will from the cable TV station had called. He'd good-naturedly begged her for a homemade meal in the past, and she'd invited him over a couple of times to eat with her and Marla. Now he was asking for dinner again. She knew that Will's parents, who were corporate types, rarely cooked, and the babysitters and housekeepers Will had grown up with weren't very good cooks, either.

"We bachelors rarely get good meals," he'd complained, sighing.

"Okay," Nicole had said impulsively, "why don't you come over Sunday for dinner?"

Afterwards, she'd told Marla and suggested that her sister invite a friend too.

"Good idea," Marla had replied. "I can make cupcakes for dessert."

"Why don't you invite that cute guy you were telling me about—Scott what's his name?"

"MacInnes," Marla supplied. "Scott MacInnes—he's a new nurse at the hospital, on the cardiac ward."

"Yes, that's the one. You said he was a little shy," Nicole pointed out. "This would be a good opportunity to get to know him better."

Marla had agreed, gotten his phone number from a mutual friend, and Scott had sounded eager to join them.

Marla had Saturday off, so they'd cleaned, and gone to their exercise club together—something they didn't usually get to do with their differing work schedules. Later they'd gone to the movies.

This morning Nicole had gotten a call from Jeremy. "My sister is a fan of your show," he'd said without preamble, "and she'd like to meet you. She'll be around late this afternoon. Can we stop in? Maybe we can order a pizza or something?"

Knowing her sister liked entertaining as much as she did, Nicole had suggested that Jeremy and Brooke join them. Jeremy had accepted the invitation with alacrity, and Nicole wondered if he'd been angling for an invitation all along.

She and Marla had dashed to the grocery for some extra food. With the drop in temperature and the end-of-September weather, she'd decided on some good, filling, autumn comfort food. She now had brisket cooking in the oven in a spicy wine sauce, with one of her favorite side dishes, lemon rice pilaf.

"Will's bringing the wine, right?" Marla asked, putting utensils in the dishwasher.

"Yes, and we have extra if it's not enough. And Jeremy said he and Brooke were capable of putting together a salad."

"And Scott's making a vegetable casserole," Marla said. "Imagine a guy who can cook! He's just gone up a lot in my estimation."

"I'm impressed," Nicole added.

She did a quick check of the brisket, basting it with the savory sauce. Everything looked fine. The rice was ready to cook at the last minute, with all the ingredients lined up. Marla was putting out the two cheeses and crackers they'd decided on for appetizers, wanting something simple so their guests would have plenty of room for dinner.

Nicole dashed upstairs and checked herself in the mirror. She was wearing jeans and a forest green top—nothing too heavy, since the kitchen would be hot. She was just smoothing her hair when the doorbell rang.

She'd told everyone five o'clock, figuring they'd eat around five thirty. It was ten of. Someone was early.

It turned out to be Will, and he handed them a bottle of good red wine. He'd barely hung up his coat when the bell rang again.

This time it was Scott, holding a simple white casserole dish.

"I made a carrot-and-zucchini casserole," he explained, handing it to Nicole. "We just have to heat it up."

She took the cover off. "Mmm, I smell fresh dill!"

"It has fresh dill?" Marla's eyebrows shot up. "You didn't tell me you're a gourmet cook, Scott!"

They'd just sat down in the living room when the bell rang again. Knowing who it was, Nicole sprang up.

"Hi!" she greeted Jeremy and Brooke brightly.

Jeremy introduced Brooke. His sister was cute and artsy looking. She wore black jeans, a golden yellow sweater, and a scarf in colors of black, yellow, and purple. Her blond hair was short and stylish.

"It's so nice to meet you," Nicole said. Jeremy handed her a large plastic bowl covered with plastic wrap. They'd brought a good-sized salad and several bottles of dressing.

"I just started watching your show and I really like it— even though I can't cook!" Brooke declared with a smile.

Nicole turned slightly to introduce everyone.

Will had risen, and his expression was delighted. "Brooke?" Nicole had never seen him look this excited.

"*William?*" Brooke's expression was one of astonishment.

Will moved over and enveloped Brooke in a gigantic hug. "Brooke!"

Nicole stared. So, she suspected, did everyone else.

Brooke moved back. "I don't believe it. William, what— how is it—"

Hastily, Nicole asked, "You two know each other?"

Brooke sent a smiling look around the room. "Very well. William was my first major boyfriend."

Brooke introduced herself and Jeremy to the others, and

they all explained who they were and how they knew Nicole and Marla.

"Wow, what a coincidence," Marla said, regarding Brooke, "you knowing Will from so long ago . . ."

"It's only twelve years since we graduated high school. I wondered why you didn't go to the reunion," Brooke told Will.

He shook his head. "I was sorry I had to miss it. I was working for another TV station, and I was on assignment in Canada for several months."

"I was sorry you weren't there too . . ."

"I'll put the salad in the refrigerator," Nicole said, and hurried into the kitchen. There were enough people staring, observing Will's and Brooke's surprise reunion.

Jeremy and his sister might not be cooks, but they had put together an attractive-looking salad, full of fresh lettuce, carrots, grape tomatoes, celery, cucumbers, and green and red peppers. Nicole replaced the wrapping and slid it into the refrigerator.

"Is there something I can help with?"

She jumped at the sound of Jeremy's voice. She hadn't heard him follow her into the kitchen.

"No thanks," she said. "Everything's almost ready."

"It smells wonderful." Jeremy's voice dropped, and he leaned over to give her a quick hug.

Even that brief gesture made her tingle, totally aware of his closeness.

They returned to the living room, where Brooke was telling everyone what a good skier and tennis player Will had been in high school, and Will, embarrassed, was trying to change the subject.

"So you guys didn't keep in touch?" Marla asked.

"William—sorry, I'm not used to calling you Will—went to college in Vermont, and I went to school in New York. We kind of drifted apart," Brooke said.

"Yeah, she had about ten guys throwing themselves at her feet," Will said.

"No, I didn't! You were busy on the ski slopes with all those girls," Brooke shot back.

But their bickering was good-natured, and soon everyone was talking about their college days.

When it was time to get the final items ready, Nicole and Marla went into the kitchen. To Nicole's surprise, the others crowded in, offering to help. Brooke was soon tossing the salad as Scott was finishing up his casserole. Nicole made the rice, and cooked celery and onions in the lemon-butter sauce, while Jeremy sliced the meat and Marla got things on the table.

By the time they sat down to dinner, they were chatting as if they'd *all* known each other in high school. Nicole was pleased as she passed around the bowl heaped with rice. Even Scott, who Marla had claimed was shy, looked relaxed and was talking almost as much as everyone else.

Jeremy dug into his brisket. "Wow, this is great."

"It's super," Will agreed.

Jeremy and Will inhaled the food as if they'd been left starving on an island for weeks. Brooke and Scott seemed to relish everything too, although they didn't eat as much or as rapidly. Nicole caught Marla's amused glance and winked at her sister.

Marla seemed to be getting along well with Scott. This dinner had been a good idea, Nicole thought. And the fact that Brooke was completely engrossed in her old boyfriend was a nice plus.

Scott was the only one who hadn't grown up in New

Jersey. He was from Connecticut, but had attended college here, liked it, and stayed.

"I'll help you clean up," Jeremy offered when they'd finished.

"Okay, then I'll make coffee and we can have Marla's dessert," Nicole said.

As they brought the first of the dishes into the kitchen, Nicole remarked to Jeremy, "I'm so glad you came. Isn't that something about Brooke and Will knowing each other! Life is full of strange coincidences!"

He smiled.

Except it wasn't a coincidence, Jeremy thought.

He was a good enough actor, though, that he was pretty sure Nicole didn't catch on when he agreed, "Yeah, life is definitely stranger than fiction."

Will had played his part to perfection. And Brooke had truly been surprised.

No one would suspect that Will and he had carefully orchestrated this whole thing at Will's request.

They'd talked twice on Saturday. First, they'd figured out the plan. Will had been asking to get a home-cooked meal at Nicole's, and Jeremy had suggested that he try to pin down a date and time during this weekend or next. When he had, Will had let Jeremy know, and Jeremy had suggested to Brooke that this might be a good Sunday to come over and try to meet Nicole.

Things had fallen into place perfectly.

And Will had promised in return not to say a word about Jeremy's famous family to Nicole. And since Brooke had promised Jeremy the same thing, it was easy to avoid the topic.

During dessert—these wonderful yellow cupcakes with

thick chocolate frosting—Will had said how much he'd enjoyed the meal. "This was great—especially since I hardly ever cook." He gave a satisfied sigh. "Would it be possible to do this again?"

"We can use my kitchen if you want," Jeremy volunteered, "as long as Nicole and Marla do the cooking."

"And Scott!" Marla interjected.

"Deal," Nicole said, and her soft, warm smile sent tingles of electricity up his spine.

They debated for a few minutes and finally settled on dinner in two weeks.

As they finished their dessert, Marla suggested a couple of rounds of the game Clue, since they had the perfect number of players. Everyone thought that was a good idea. It seemed no one wanted the evening to end.

They played four games. Scott won the first, Jeremy the second, and Marla the third. Jeremy won the fourth game, and was declared by everyone to be the master.

Scott glanced at his watch. "I'd better go," he said, the reluctance in his voice evident. "I have an early morning at the hospital tomorrow."

"I have to get up early too," Nicole said.

"So do I," Jeremy added.

As they put away the game and got their coats, Jeremy overheard his sister and Will exchanging cell phone numbers and making plans for the following weekend. Scott and Marla seemed to be pretty cozy too. This was his chance to talk to Nicole.

She must have read his mind. "So, do you want to come over on Friday and sample the meal for the show the week after?"

"You couldn't keep me away," he answered. "What's for dinner?"

"I'm not sure yet." Her chocolate-brown eyes sparkled. "But it will be delicious, I promise."

"I can't wait," he said.

"Friday's only a few days away," she reminded him.

Will and Scott both left, and then Brooke said good night.

"I'll walk you to your car," Jeremy said to his sister.

Marla smiled. "Well, I don't have to go into work until four o'clock tomorrow. I'm staying up late and catching up on this week's episodes of my favorite soaps."

Jeremy froze. He tried not to show the sudden fear that clutched him.

"What soaps do you watch?" Brooke asked easily.

Boy, his sister was almost as good an actress as their mother. She sounded merely curious.

"I follow *As the Universe Spins* and *Medical Center.* Recently I started watching *All My Relatives* also," Marla answered.

"Oh, I like to watch *All My Relatives* too," Brooke said. "Do you watch soaps too?" she asked Nicole innocently.

Jeremy's heart was pounding. Why didn't his sister leave well enough alone and try to change the topic? He contemplated ways to kill her.

Nicole was shaking her head. "No, I'm not into them. I like some of the nighttime shows, like *Heroes* and *Lost.* And of course I love the cooking shows! My favorite is *Chef vs. Chef.*"

"Oh, that's a fun show," Brooke said. "Even people like me, who can't cook, like that show."

Jeremy quietly let out a long breath.

He pulled on his jacket, then turned to Nicole and gave her a quick kiss. "I'll see you on Friday," he whispered.

She stood on her toes and kissed him back. "See you Friday." She smiled.

He left with Brooke. Once across the street, Brooke unlocked her car and placed what was left of the salad inside.

"You took a chance talking about *All My Relatives*," Jeremy said accusingly.

"It would have looked strange if I hadn't at least continued the conversation," Brooke said.

Jeremy made a huffing noise, then dropped the subject. At least no harm had been done. "So you're going to see Will again?" he asked.

"Yes." A dreamy expression crossed her face, and then she frowned. "It was a good thing he didn't say anything either."

"Yeah, we'd better warn him," Jeremy said, striving to keep a straight face.

Brooke regarded him. "Really, Jeremy, if you keep seeing Nicole, you're going to have to tell her sometime. It's better if you don't wait too long. She could find out from someone else."

That thought bugged him as his sister drove away.

Chapter Seven

Okay, spill it," Kathy said.

"Why do you think I have something to spill?" Nicole asked as she walked briskly on the treadmill.

But Kathy, on the next treadmill, persisted. "I know you, Nicki. Something's up. You've been smiling more than usual, and I caught you humming after fifth period—despite it being a crazy day today."

The two were exercising on Tuesday afternoon at the local gym. It had been a particularly rough day of teaching. The kids had seemed hyper—maybe it was the weather, since a storm had been brewing all day. Nicole had had to calm down one student, then another. One was worried about what someone said about her hair, and the other about her grade on the math test from the previous period. And then there were several who were just generally restless.

Still, she'd felt upbeat most of the day, although she was relieved when the last class ended and she could meet Kathy at the gym.

Nicole's best friends from high school and college now

lived in southern New Jersey and Pennsylvania, respectively. Kathy was her closest friend from work. A history teacher who had started teaching the same year as Nicole, Kathy had grown up in East Brunswick, a more crowded town in central New Jersey. The two had hit it off right away and become close friends.

"Come on," Kathy urged. "Tell me what's up."

Nicole smiled. "Guess I can't fool you." She went on to tell Kathy about Jeremy and the whole "boyfriend" thing on her cooking show.

"The episode with Jeremy is going to air on Friday," Nicole said. "You'll get to see him."

"He sounds great! So, why do I sense you're a little worried?"

"Because what if he's like Brad? Jeremy grew up in a wealthy community, in Short Hills."

Kathy whistled. She knew about the whole thing with Brad. She'd seen how hurt Nicole had been over her former boyfriend's betrayal.

"Doctor Antonio Perez—gee, that does sound vaguely familiar," Kathy said slowly. "He must be a well-known doctor. Anyway, Nicole—" She paused as their treadmills stopped at almost the same time. "There's no reason to believe he'll be just like Brad! I say you give him a chance."

Nicole wiped her forehead with a towel. "I'm scared," she admitted bluntly. "My family is normal, strictly middle-class. I'm proud of them, of course," she rushed on. "But Jeremy's, well, probably rich, used to mixing with the elite members of society . . ."

"Not everyone thinks in such a close-minded way," Kathy said, "except maybe for Brad and his family. My cousin's best friend grew up in a middle-class family, and she married a millionaire from Boston."

"Still, that's not the norm," Nicole pointed out. "People from the upper class usually socialize with their own."

"Has he acted like he looks down on you in any way?" Kathy challenged.

"No," Nicole admitted.

"Then, what's the problem? Why don't you go out with him and just have fun?" Kathy paused, and sighed. "I wish things were as simple with me and Kurt." Kathy had been dating her boyfriend on and off for a year.

Maybe she should take Kathy's advice, Nicole thought as they went to work out on some other equipment. Maybe she should simply have a good time with Jeremy.

She'd wanted to speak to Marla about her concerns, but her sister was working the late shift this week. Also, she suspected her thoughts were busy with Scott—and Nicole didn't want to detract from that. Marla had been hurt in the past, and hadn't been this interested in a guy in ages. She'd spoken a lot about Scott during the last couple of days.

By the time Nicole and Kathy finished exercising, showered, and changed, it was almost dinner time. They drove to a place nearby and had sandwiches and soup for dinner. When they got out it was starting to rain.

They parted, Kathy to go to her apartment nearby and Nicole to her house. Since she was on the cooking show and had plenty of work to do for that, she no longer taught her adult school class on Tuesdays. She drove straight home through the rain.

The house was dark and quiet when she arrived. Once inside, Nicole threw in a load of wash, checked her mail and e-mail, and settled down with a romance novel she'd picked up the previous week.

She couldn't help glancing out the window several times at Jeremy's house across the street.

The house was dark, and his van wasn't parked in the driveway. She recalled then that he'd said something to Brooke on Sunday about meeting her for dinner on Tuesday. He must still be out with his sister.

A couple of times she heard cars driving down the street through the pinging of the steady rain. When she heard a door slam nearby, she couldn't help herself. She got up from the chair she was sitting in and peeked out the window.

Jeremy was dashing up his sidewalk through the rain. Within seconds he was inside his house, and lights were going on.

Nicole sighed and went back to her book. She shouldn't be watching him, she chastised herself. His comings and goings were his own business.

Two minutes later her cell phone rang.

"Nicole? It's Jeremy." His voice sounded husky and appealing.

She scooted down further into the deep chair. "Hi," she said softly. "How are you?"

"I'm okay. I've been busy." There was a pause, and she could picture him sitting on a chair just like she was, maybe running his hand through his thick dark hair. "I'm trying to get wiring done on a new office condo."

She told him a little about her hectic day at work. Somehow it sounded amusing as she related the events of the day. Or maybe she just felt better after speaking about it.

"Well . . . ," he said after a few minutes. "I ate supper tonight with Brooke. The restaurant's food wasn't half as good as yours."

Delight spurted through her at his words. "Thanks!"

"I can't wait till Friday."

They spoke for a few more minutes, and then Jeremy said good night.

Nicole closed her phone slowly. She felt tired but content. Jeremy was looking forward to Friday.

And so was she.

"Ms. Vitarelli, there's a visitor for you in the front hallway," said the school aide over the PA system.

Surprised, Nicole got up from her desk. School had been dismissed five minutes before, and students were still in the halls, the walkers milling about, the bus students rushing from lockers to the stairways. The noise of kids calling to each other and lockers slamming echoed through the long corridors.

Nicole proceeded down the stairs, wondering who her visitor was. It must be Marla, she decided. Her sister had today, Thursday, off from work. Who else could it be? Marla had met her here once when they were going to drop off her car for repairs, so she was familiar with the school, but what was she doing here now? She hoped it wasn't an emergency.

She hurried down the second flight, and then practically ran down the main hallway to the front area . . . and stopped.

By the sign-in desk, Jeremy waited, hands in his jeans pockets, an olive green sweater outlining his masculine shoulders.

"Jeremy?"

"Hey, Nicole." He flashed his warm smile and she felt her insides melt. "I hope you don't mind my stopping in here."

"Is everything okay?" she asked. Several thirteen-year-old girls hanging around nearby were ogling him.

"Yeah, I just thought I'd surprise you and offer to take you out for dinner."

She drew closer, returning his smile. "What a great offer! I am surprised. But it's kind of early." It was only a few minutes after three o'clock.

"I thought you could show me around your building, and then I'd show you the office I'm working on." His smile warmed her.

"I'd love to," she said promptly. "I can't leave the building yet, but I can show you around."

She signed Jeremy into the visitor list, and then, conscious of curious looks from both staff and students who had stayed for after-school activities, she gave him the tour. She showed him the updated theater and music wing, which he said was impressive; the cafeteria and gym; and a variety of different classrooms.

"So this one is yours," he said, looking at the room, which she'd decorated with bright bulletin boards, fake fall leaves, and some Halloween items. "Now when I picture you at work I can envision where you are."

A little shiver of delight skittered up Nicole's spine. It was like biting into ice cream, cold but delicious. *Jeremy spent time picturing her at work.*

The halls had grown much quieter, except for the sweeping of a janitor's broom. A group of the middle school cheerleaders were practicing outside not far from her window, and their cheers could be heard even though her window was now closed against the cool autumn breeze. While it was sunny, the temperature had dropped during the last few days, typical for the first day of October.

By this time, it was three-thirty, and okay for the staff to leave. "So, where will I picture you working?" Nicole asked as she gathered her jacket and her bag that held papers to correct.

"Come on. I'll show you. It's in our town, right on Route Forty-six."

She turned out the lights and then led Jeremy downstairs. He signed out while she hung up her keys.

She paused to give Kathy a quick call to tell her she wouldn't be going to exercise today.

"I heard you had a male visitor," Kathy said with a chuckle.

Nicole sighed. Was nothing secret around here?

"Good for you. That's more important than exercise. Enjoy the time with him!" Kathy finished.

She didn't call Marla. Her sister had told her she and Scott were going out for dinner, since neither was working today. Nicole was glad. Scott seemed like a nice guy, and although he was quieter than Marla, that didn't seem to bother her sister.

Nicole followed Jeremy's *Lightning Fast* van as he drove to the building with the office condos back in Mount Olive. Once there, he gave her the tour of the office, which a dentist was buying.

There was another guy there whom Jeremy knew, measuring for cabinets, and they briefly said hello.

"Here's the basic electric panel," Jeremy said, showing it to her. He went on to point out the wiring he'd been doing.

While he talked, Nicole observed how animated Jeremy was. He really loved his job and took pride in his work. She'd met many other guys who didn't enjoy their jobs— they were bored, or frustrated because they either weren't doing what they wanted or had grown to dislike their jobs. But Jeremy radiated an enthusiasm and pride in his work that was appealing.

"I'm glad you showed me this," she said, turning to gaze up at him.

"I'm glad you're glad." He slung an arm around her, grinning. She leaned into his embrace.

"What do you say we get something to eat?" he asked.

Jeremy had suggested they go to the Budd Lake Diner, and Nicole agreed quickly, saying how much she liked their food. They ate hamburgers and fries, and Jeremy felt relaxed and happy in her company.

It had been an impulse to go over to her school and see if she'd want to eat dinner out, but he was glad she'd agreed.

And so far, she gave no sign that she knew anything more about him than what he'd told her.

Of course, Brooke had warned him again on Tuesday that he'd have to tell her about their family if he kept seeing Nicole. But he'd assured his sister it was too soon to reveal the truth.

"Not yet," he'd said to her. "I want Nicole to get to know the real me before springing our rich—and famous—family on her. I want to be liked for *myself*." His voice had sounded imploring. "For once in my life, I want to be judged for who I am without anything else getting in the way."

Brooke had sighed. "I understand."

"You don't have to worry about Will," he'd added. "He already knows us and has for years. He knows *you*."

She'd sent him a look he couldn't decipher.

So far he liked Nicole a lot, and he wanted to get to know her even better. But he worried: what if she was like Monica? What if she liked him mostly for money and prestige?

She must have some awareness that he was far from poverty-stricken. Although he worked hard for his money, and had bought his house himself, she knew that he came from an upper-class community and that he had a second car—not something every single guy could afford. She *didn't* know he'd been on a lot of vacations, and he certainly had no intention of discussing the investments he had—money in the bank and the small house he'd bought only a few blocks away, which he rented out.

But any awareness she had wasn't changing her behavior. So far she appeared simply interested in him. And he'd like to keep it that way.

After dinner he followed her car back to their street. Practically jumping from his van, he met her and walked her to her front door.

The evening had grown colder. He saw a blind flicker in Mrs. Kelly's front window. She was watching her neighbors again. He could smell the tang of wood burning in a fireplace, and saw smoke coming from the chimney two doors down from Nicole's home.

"Want to have a cup of cocoa?" she asked as she fished in her purse for her keys.

"That sounds good."

She opened her door. The lights in her living room were on, but dimly.

"Oh, ah, sorry!" he heard her say.

Walking into the living room, he saw Nicole's sister Marla slide to one end of the couch, away from Scott.

Their entrance had obviously interrupted some private time. Marla's face was flushed. He had a pretty good hunch she and Scott had been kissing.

"We were—ah—going to have some hot cocoa," Nicole said quickly. "Do you guys want some?"

"No thanks," Marla said.

"Sure," Scott responded at the exact same moment.

Marla and Scott looked at each other and laughed suddenly. Nicole was smiling, her chocolatey eyes sparkling in the low light. Jeremy suppressed his own desire to laugh, and merely smiled.

"Um . . . I guess we'll have some," Marla said.

Nicole went into the kitchen and Jeremy followed, giving the other couple some privacy.

Nicole grimaced. "I guess that was bad timing." She shrugged out of her jacket and he took his own off.

"It happens sometimes," Jeremy said. "It could be us next." He leaned down and gave her a quick kiss.

Nicole gave a low laugh. "I guess so." She went over to the pantry and pulled out a box of hot cocoa. "You don't mind a mix, do you?"

"I don't have the slightest idea how to make it from scratch," he told her honestly. Never mind that when skiing in Colorado he'd probably had some of the best cocoa or hot chocolate around. He'd still rather have it here, with Nicole, homemade or not. "I don't think I'd even know the difference."

"I do know how to make it from scratch," she said suddenly. "And you *would* taste the difference."

He looked at her. There was the smallest amount of something—anxiety?—on her face.

"I don't care if it's homemade or not," he continued. "I'll just enjoy having it with you."

She smiled, and he saw her posture relax.

Marla and Scott entered the room. They sat down at the table, and soon they were all sipping the hot cocoa, talking about football and the Giants' chances of having a winning season.

A little while later, Jeremy stifled a yawn. He caught Nicole watching him.

"Sorry," he said. "I was up early working on that office. I'd better call it a night."

"I have to get up early too," she agreed.

She walked him to the door. After he'd slid his arms into his jacket, he leaned forward and gave her a quick kiss. "So I'll see you tomorrow, at my place?" He thought it was neat that she wanted to try cooking in his kitchen.

"Yes. About five-thirty?" she asked.

"That's great." As he departed, he found himself thinking not just about Friday's meal, but also about Nicole, her soft lips, her warm smile, and her lively personality.

Nicole went upstairs and got ready for sleep. She looked at the tote bag containing the papers that needed correcting, and decided to do them tomorrow during her prep time.

She found herself sighing. She really liked Jeremy. She thought he liked her too.

And he absolutely loved her cooking.

Was it her destiny to have men like her for her looks— like Brad—or for her cooking? While it was nice to be appreciated for both those factors, she wanted to be liked because she was a caring person as well.

She was still pondering the idea a few minutes later when she heard Scott leave, and Marla came upstairs.

"Did you have a nice evening?" she asked as Marla stuck her head in the doorway.

"Yes," Marla answered, a dreamy note in her voice. "How about you?"

"Yes. I'm sorry I interrupted you guys kissing . . ."

Marla shrugged. "Speaking about kissing—how's Jeremy?"

"What?"

"How is he? Is he a good kisser?" Her sister was grinning, a mischievous glint in her eyes.

"Yes . . . ," Nicole admitted. "How about Scott?" she shot back.

Marla smiled. "Yes!"

All of Friday, Nicole was busy at work, but despite that, she was full of anticipation about going to Jeremy's house—and not just because she wanted to cook in that dream kitchen.

When she got home, she changed to jeans and a long-sleeved aqua T-shirt, and organized the things she had to bring over. She carried over some pots and rang his doorbell.

"Hi!" he greeted her, opening the door immediately. "Let me help you."

It took only one more trip to bring the utensils and food she needed.

"I'm glad you're cooking here," he said. "I can actually watch."

Nicole let her glance sweep the spacious kitchen, the granite counters, the wide stainless steel sink. "This is going to be a real pleasure—not that it isn't anyway," she added, "but wow, this kitchen is super!"

He pulled up one of the kitchen stools and watched as she began combining spices to dip the chicken cutlets in.

They talked about their days at work. Nicole's had been busy, but the kids had been calmer, fortunately, than they had earlier in the week.

She didn't tell Jeremy that several of the kids had asked

if she had a boyfriend—to which she'd replied that Jeremy was just a good friend. Why start gossip?

"He's cute. He should be your boyfriend," Jamie, one of her students had declared. Several other girls had nodded sagely.

Jeremy described how he'd worked on the wiring job for the dentist, and then had visited two potential customers and worked up estimates for their jobs.

As she finished coating her special spicy baked chicken, Jeremy said suddenly, "I should be helping. Is there something I can do?"

"I'm going to make that lemon-and-pepper rice again, the one I made on Sunday," Nicole said. She'd noticed that Jeremy had eaten a lot of it. "Want to cut up some onions and celery?"

Jeremy agreed, and she showed him how she wanted them cut, and then how to make the basic instant rice that she used in the dish.

Working side by side with him was cozy and satisfying. Cutting up vegetables, talking, the local radio station playing some oldies in the background . . . it felt natural—like they had been doing this kind of thing together for a long time.

She could get used to this, she thought. Then she chastised herself. She shouldn't assume this was anything more than a friendly, cooking-and-eating relationship.

Except there'd been those kisses!

When there was nothing left to do but the last-minute warming of the rice and microwaving carrots, Jeremy set a bottle of wine on the table to accompany their meal. They went into the family room and sat on the couch.

Wind rattled the windows. The sky was partly cloudy, and the October wind was making the temperature feel cooler than yesterday. The trees in his backyard were beginning to turn color and were showing off their leaves in tones of red, orange, and golden yellow.

"It's beautiful outside," Nicole said. "I love fall, and it always looks so gorgeous around here."

Jeremy nodded. "I agree. And there are more trees here then where I grew up, so I can really appreciate the beauty of nature here."

"Didn't you like growing up in Millburn?" she asked, testing the waters. He didn't frequently speak about his hometown.

He shrugged. "It's a pretty area, for Essex County— not as crowded or urban as some of the other towns. But it's kind of—" He paused. "Well, let's just say I like it out here a lot better. The people are more down-to-earth."

She nodded, sipping her Diet Pepsi.

"How about you?" he asked. "Did you like Parsippany?"

"Yes," she answered, "although it's more crowded there than in Mount Olive. I like it here better too."

"Yeah, it's great to have more space around you," he said. "Here we have the lake and open space. We do have a couple of parks in Millburn, but it's definitely more congested, and that's even . . ."

"Even?" she prompted when he hesitated.

"And that's even among some of the really big houses. Although"—he grinned, waggling his eyebrows like Groucho Marx—"space is good, but sometimes"—he scooted closer on the couch—"you want to be close, right?"

Nicole tilted her head up, and he had just touched his lips to hers when the buzzer went off, signaling that the chicken was nearly done.

"Oh, I have to check the chicken," she said, pulling

back, wishing she'd had another couple of minutes to enjoy his kiss.

They soon had dinner on the table. Jeremy appeared to enjoy this meal as much as the suppers she'd cooked previously. He lingered over the chicken, savoring the flavors and telling her several times how good everything was.

"I have a surprise for you," she said when they were almost finished. "I made a chocolate mousse earlier and left it in my refrig. It's light, so whenever you want to eat it I'll bring it over."

"It sounds wonderful," he said, giving a satisfied sigh. "Let's take a little break, then have it."

He pitched in with the cleanup without being asked. For someone who had grown up in a wealthy home, he certainly didn't mind helping, she observed.

They went over to her house for dessert. When she placed the chocolate mousses on the dining room table, she found Jeremy in the living room, staring at a photo of her, Marla, and their brother Joe.

"Nice photo," he said.

"It was taken at Marla's graduation from college a couple of years ago," she said.

They sat down and Jeremy oohed and ahhed over the dessert. Finishing, he licked his spoon loudly. "This was amazing. And just think, I get to eat it all over again next week on the show!"

Something tightened inside Nicole at his words.

Was he looking forward to eating more than he was to seeing her?

Nicole was in the middle of setting up her ingredients and utensils in the studio when Jeremy walked in, a little early.

She looked at him, surprised.

He wore a nice outfit again—dark blue shirt, black pants, and a blue, green, black, and gold tie. He looked so handsome, her insides turned as mushy as oatmeal.

"Hi," he greeted her, and leaned down to give her a brief kiss.

Now her insides flipped.

She hadn't seen him since Saturday, when they'd gone to the movies with Marla and Scott. Brooke, he told her, had gone into the city with Will for the day. "But they still want to do dinner with us soon," he'd assured her.

The movie had been entertaining—a goofy comedy—and afterwards they'd come back to her place and had apple pie that Marla had baked. But they hadn't really spent time alone.

The week had been busy at work, with back-to-school night and a cooking club Nicole had started for interested students. Jeremy had called twice.

Even though she hadn't seen him all week, Jeremy had occupied Nicole's thoughts. She'd be erasing the chalkboard or collecting papers, and suddenly she'd picture his smiling face. Or while folding clothes or brushing her teeth she'd recall how husky his voice had sounded when he spoke about looking forward to seeing her on Friday.

She'd coordinated with him and was wearing a medium-length black skirt and a blue top. It was cold enough outside for a sweater, but inside the studio it was usually warm because of the bright lights. Even in her light top, she could feel herself growing warm from that one quick kiss.

"Mmm . . . ," he said, and stepping closer, reached out and pulled her to him. "I missed you," he whispered, and this time the kiss was longer.

Now she felt really warm.

Conscious that Will and Shelly were bustling around, Nicole stepped back. "I have to finish setting up." She heard the reluctance in her voice.

She completed the set-up, and they began taping right on time. Nicole mentioned Jeremy at least four times, speaking about how much he liked the recipes from last week. Irene and Shelly both sounded pleased when they took a short break.

"You're incorporating mentions of Jeremy in just the right places," Irene praised.

Before she knew it, Nicole was lighting dark green candles and she and Jeremy were sitting down at a table set in autumn colors of forest green and gold with touches of orange.

"Everything smells so good, I can't wait to eat!" Jeremy declared for the benefit of the audience who would be watching the episode.

They concluded the segment with Jeremy sampling everything and describing the superior flavors to the TV audience. As Will backed up at the end, Jeremy reached out and gave Nicole a big hug. "Sweetheart, your cooking is the best," he declared.

"Cut!" Shelly's voice sounded triumphant. "That was great, guys!"

"Now we can relax," Nicole said in a low voice to Jeremy.

"I am relaxed." He grinned. "And I'm happy—although I want to finish my portions." He indicated the plate, which was still almost full.

He did look relaxed, she thought.

"That was a great show, guys." There was clapping nearby, and Amanda, the star of another cooking show the station hosted, rose from her seat in the audience area. "I just stopped in to talk to Thomas and stayed to watch the taping. I'm keeping these recipes, Nicole."

"Thanks." Nicole liked Amanda, a young widow who had a show on cooking fast and simple family-friendly meals.

Irene had moved forward. "Speaking of Thomas . . . he's still here, and he wants to see you, Nicole."

Nicole's eyebrows shot up. She didn't see Thomas around too often. If he was still here in the late afternoons or evenings when she taped, he was almost always on the phone.

"Who's Thomas?" Jeremy asked, lifting a forkful of the spicy chicken.

"He's the executive producer," Nicole answered, with a slight frown. *What did he want?*

"Oh, it's good news," Irene reassured her.

"Okay, I'll go see him. You can keep eating," she said to Jeremy. She wanted to finish her own meal, but was curious to see what Thomas wanted.

Thomas Clarkson, the executive producer, was a distinguished-looking man in his fifties. He'd gone gray young, yet it hadn't detracted from his handsome face. Nicole knew from Irene that Thomas was a shrewd businessman with a knack for knowing what audiences wanted.

When she approached his office, the door was ajar. He was on the computer, not the phone, and looked up when she entered.

"Hello, Nicole!" He sounded excited.

"Hello, Thomas," she responded, smiling.

"I have some good news," he said, waving her to the chair in front of his desk.

"What's that?" she asked, sitting down in the comfortable chair.

He braced his hands on the desk. "Since your boyfriend appeared on the show that aired last week, we've been getting a lot of positive feedback. A lot of our viewers have e-mailed—some even called—to say how much they enjoyed seeing him and that they thought it was a good idea. Many people said they're getting their boyfriends and husbands to watch the next one—the one you taped tonight—when it airs next week."

Nicole smiled, relieved. "That's good," she said. "More viewers are always a good thing."

"You bet!" He clapped his hands. "More viewers—and a larger percentage of male viewers—will attract more advertising dollars." Seeing her expression, he added, "Don't look at me like that. I know men and women should be treated equally. But the advertisers are always looking for a larger audience, and if your show appeals to not just women, but men too, we can up our ad prices—and they'll pay it."

Nicole was familiar with the way it worked. She'd had a discussion with Thomas and Irene about this once before. "Well, it sounds good," she said, figuring she could leave and join Jeremy.

"So that's why I want to kick this up a notch," he continued.

Nicole paused. "Kick this up a notch?" She hated to sound like a parrot, but she wasn't sure what Thomas meant.

"Yes." He beamed at her. "On the next show, I want you to have your boyfriend help you with the cooking."

Chapter Eight

Jeremy ate slowly, savoring the flavors of Nicole's spicy chicken, baked potato, and sweet carrots. Later he'd enjoy the dessert.

He wondered if there was a problem. She'd been speaking to the executive producer for at least ten minutes. Part of the studio was now dark, and people seemed to be finishing tasks, packing things away.

As he put down his fork and knife, he heard the click of her shoes. A few seconds later she came into view.

The expression on her beautiful face was concerned.

Behind her, a man in his late fifties followed. He smiled at Jeremy, a congenial smile.

Nicole introduced him. "This is Thomas Clarkson, our executive producer."

"Nice to meet you," Jeremy said, standing and shaking the other man's hand.

"Likewise. Nicole will explain the change in the next show," Thomas said, and then continued on to another part of the studio. "Irene? Do you have a moment?"

Jeremy looked at Nicole again.

Her cheeks were flushed.

"Is everything okay?" he asked.

"Yes," she said slowly. "But . . . Thomas wants to change something for next time—and maybe from now on." A small frown appeared on her face.

"What?" he asked. He hoped they didn't want him off the show. He liked doing it. This wasn't acting. This was real—and fun! Besides sampling Nicole's cooking, he got to spend time with her.

She sighed. "They want you to help cook on the next show."

"They do?" That was a surprise.

"Yes. You see, they got a lot of good feedback when you appeared the first time. Now Thomas figures we'll get more of a male audience, and with more men watching, we'll have a bigger market share—and they can earn more advertising dollars for the show."

"Oh." He knew something about advertising dollars and TV from conversations with his mother. What she said made sense.

"Do you mind?" she asked.

He recognized anxiety in her eyes. Leaning down, he dropped his voice low. "No, I don't mind at all." He caught a faint whiff of a fruity cologne surrounding her.

Instantly, relief replaced the anxiety on her face. "Are you sure?" Her voice was hopeful.

"Yes. I think I'm capable of learning a few things, like simple cooking techniques."

"Oh, I'm sure you are!" she agreed. She gave him a brilliant smile. "Thanks, Jeremy. That's the way I'd like to handle it—you'll be helping me as I demonstrate and learning with the audience."

"It's no problem." At least he hoped it wouldn't be. But . . . with a larger role on the show, what if someone called to say they recognized the youngest child of soap star Sharon Maloney?

Nicole stepped closer, placed her hands on his shoulders, and stood on tiptoes. "Thank you, Jeremy." She kissed him.

Electrical sparks skittered throughout his being as if they were barreling through a cable. All he could think was, *Wow.* He forgot what he was supposed to be worrying about.

"There they go again." Shelly's voice broke the intensity of the moment. Nicole stepped back.

"We're almost done packing it in here," Shelly continued cheerfully.

"Okay. We'll get this stuff out of the kitchen," Nicole said quickly, waving at the food and pots and pans. Her cheeks were flushed a pretty pink.

Jeremy pitched in, and they soon had everything in shopping bags and loaded up Nicole's car.

"You're sure you don't mind cooking on the next few shows?" There was still a hint of uncertainty in her eyes.

"I don't mind. It might be fun."

Yeah, it might be fun as long as no one recognized him, he added silently.

Brooke surprised everyone by calling on Saturday and saying her dad had six tickets to the Giants' football game on Sunday, but that he and her mom were going to a wedding on Long Island and couldn't use the tickets.

"Wow, it's nice to know people!" Marla remarked. "I'll bet her father treated one of the team members."

"She said he does go to a lot of the games," Nicole said. "Do you think Sunday afternoon is okay for Scott?"

"I'm calling him right now."

They had originally planned to make dinner on Sunday, but the plans swiftly changed to a brunch so that they could all get to the game.

"Hmm . . . do you think we should have considered tailgating?" Marla asked.

Nicole shook her head. "I don't know if we have all the correct equipment to cook and keep the food warm, and besides, Brooke suggested a brunch would work out perfectly for her, Jeremy, and Will."

"We'd better work on the menu and get to the store if we need anything extra," Marla said, glancing at her watch. She picked up the phone.

They soon had the menu set. Nicole would make homemade waffles and fry up some bacon; Marla would make corn muffins and cranberry-orange muffins; and they would provide coffee and tea. Jeremy and Brooke would bring bagels and cream cheese; Will would bring orange and grapefruit juices and all the paper goods; and Scott volunteered to bring eggs and vegetables and to make omelets to order.

"Sounds like a great menu," Brooke said when Nicole called her back. "I'll tell Jeremy when he gets here."

Jeremy had told her after the TV show that he was spending part of Saturday doing some work for Brooke on her stage set at the college and that afterward he had to go over to a house that was having some electrical problems. He'd asked if she minded just hanging out on Saturday and watching a movie with him.

Did she mind? Nicole was thrilled.

Nicole and Marla got to work doing a rapid cleaning. Marla and Scott were both working the three-to-eleven shift at the hospital, so Nicole volunteered to pick up the extra items they needed later in the afternoon when the Saturday rush at the grocery was over. She got down to working on her lesson plans and grading papers, and before she knew it Marla was leaving.

She ran over to the food store, then came back and finished grading the last of the papers. At four o'clock Jeremy called to say he was running late. "I just got a call from a friend of a friend who needs an estimate on a room he's finishing in his basement," he told her. "I probably won't get there till five-thirty."

"No problem," she said lightly. She didn't mind having some time to relax—and spend a little extra time on her hair and makeup.

It was almost six o'clock when Jeremy got to her house. He did look tired, she thought, but his face glowed when she opened the door. Was it seeing her—or just satisfaction from a job well done? Maybe it was a little of both.

"Hi," she murmured, and he swooped her into a big hug, then a loud kiss.

"I'm glad to see you," he said.

They'd agreed to have a pizza delivered—Sicilian this time—and Nicole had made a salad with her own Italian dressing. Afterward, Jeremy helped her set the table for the following day's brunch, and then they cuddled on her couch and watched a fun adventure movie that Nicole had in her collection. They'd both seen the movie before, but not for a long time.

Near the end of the movie, she saw Jeremy's eyes grow heavy, and as the ending music blared and the credits rolled, she heard a slight snore escape his lips. He was fast asleep.

Nicole lowered the volume on the TV and draped a fleece throw over him. The lights were already dim, and she re-settled next to him on the couch. She'd let him sleep for a while. *Chef vs. Chef* was coming on soon, and she'd wake him after that.

The chefs were cooking five dishes each that included the day's secret ingredient, pumpkin. She watched with interest as they created everything from pumpkin soup and chicken with pumpkin sauce, to pumpkin pies and pumpkin ice cream.

Marla came in just before the show ended. She wore a satisfied smile on her face. Nicole suspected her happy expression had something to do with Scott.

Nicole put her finger to her lips as Jeremy stirred.

Marla smiled. "He looks cute," she whispered.

"I'll wake him when the show is over," Nicole whispered back. "How was work?"

"It wasn't too bad. We have a new set of preemie twins, born this morning."

"Did you get to see Scott at work?" Nicole asked.

Marla's smile grew wider. "Yes, we ate a quick dinner together." She yawned, and went into the kitchen to get a snack. A few minutes later she went upstairs.

Nicole watched the end of the show, and then turned off the TV. She gently shook Jeremy's shoulder.

"Wake up, Jeremy," she said in a low voice.

He opened his eyes slowly, and stared at her, disoriented. "What is it?"

"You fell asleep," she told him softly.

He sat up abruptly. "Shoot, I'm sorry."

"It's okay. You must have been beat. You didn't even hear Marla come in."

"I am tired." He stood up. "I'd better go get a good

night's sleep. I'll see you in the morning." He pulled her into his arms and gave her a gentle, sleepy kiss.

But even that sent sparks from her lips to her toes.

"Look at this." Marla said to Nicole, helping Scott pull ingredients from two bags. "We've got fresh mushrooms, green and red peppers, onions, basil, tomatoes . . ."

"I'm impressed," Nicole said lightly as she stirred her waffle batter. The smell of freshly brewed coffee surrounded them.

Scott took out two cartons of eggs and several bags of shredded cheddar cheese. He looked cute—kind of shy and almost embarrassed by their compliments. "Omelets aren't that hard to make."

That might be true, but Nicole and Marla didn't know too many guys who cooked.

Not that she thought less of Jeremy because he didn't really cook. In fact, she respected him for being a good sport and agreeing to learn on her show. She just hoped that, after their first session, he would still be agreeable.

Watching the glow on her sister's face now as she and Scott bent their heads close together, Nicole knew it wasn't just cooking that was attracting Marla to Scott. No, her sister really liked the guy.

Within a few minutes the doorbell rang and Will arrived, closely followed by Brooke and Jeremy.

"Sorry I fell asleep last night," Jeremy whispered as he gave her a big hug.

"It's okay," Nicole said lightly. Even a friendly hug from Jeremy had her growing as warm as an oven.

Scott was taking omelet orders and was soon whipping up several as Nicole made the waffles. Soon, they were all sitting down to a bountiful breakfast as they debated the Giants' chances of winning the football game.

Nicole didn't know too much about football, but she enjoyed the camaraderie among them all. When Will admitted he liked the opposing team, he took the ribbing with a good-natured smile.

"This is delicious," Jeremy said, helping himself to another waffle. "And that cheese-and-pepper omelet was great," he complimented Scott.

Scott was still the quietest of the bunch, but Nicole observed his eyes were usually fastened on Marla. And he did talk to her more than to anyone else.

They really like each other! she thought, and felt a rush of gladness for her sister. Scott was nice and intelligent and seemed considerate, and it certainly looked like her sister was happy around him.

After their leisurely breakfast, everyone cleaned up together and got ready to leave for the stadium.

Although the day was a beautiful fall one and comfortably warm, Nicole knew the stadium could get cool, especially if it got windy. She was wearing a long-sleeved T-shirt but packed up a sweatshirt, and they brought a few blankets and vinyl stadium seat covers with them. It had been decided that they would take two cars to the game, since no one could fit all six people in one car. Besides, Will and Brooke were thinking of visiting someone they knew who lived near the stadium after the game.

Scott might have been the quietest at the breakfast table, but it quickly became apparent that in the stadium he was one of the loudest. The Giants started out strongly, scoring a touchdown early in the game. Scott's voice reverberated as he yelled.

Jeremy yelled almost as loudly, and Nicole found herself screaming along with the rest of them.

Towards the end of the first quarter, the other team scored, and suddenly the game got more competitive. Nicole enjoyed sitting beside Jeremy, his arm slung around her, both watching intently and then yelling when the Giants advanced, groaning when they fumbled.

They were both full from the big breakfast, but toward the end of the second quarter Jeremy said he was going to get a soda and asked if she wanted one.

"I'll go with you," Nicole said, wanting to stretch her legs. Their seats weren't bad, but even her short legs could feel cramped in the stadium. "It was really nice of your dad to give us these tickets."

"Yeah, he's a good guy." Jeremy guided her to the refreshment stands.

They got their sodas, and Jeremy added some fries. Turning to go back to their friends, Nicole heard someone call out, "Jeremy!"

Approaching them was a man as tall as Jeremy with bright red hair. Jeremy took one look at him and let out a whoop. "Sean! How are you, man?"

The two did the whole male thing, slapping each other on the back, while Nicole stood by, amused.

"So, how are you?" the guy named Sean repeated.

"I'm great, just great! How about you?"

"Oh, I'm fine!" Sean cast a curious look at Nicole.

"Oh! Sorry, Nicole, this is Sean O'Leary, a college buddy of mine. Sean, this is Nicole Vitarelli." As he said the words, she saw a slight shadow pass over Jeremy's face.

They shook hands, and then Jeremy told her, "I haven't seen Sean for a couple of years." Turning to Sean, he asked, "Are you still living in Cincinnati?"

"No, I moved back to New York—I'm living in Brooklyn now. I've been meaning to call you but we only moved back last month . . ."

Nicole said hastily, "I'll leave you two to talk." She had a feeling that Jeremy really wanted to spend a little time with his friend.

She also had a feeling that Jeremy wanted her gone. Why, she wasn't quite sure—but he'd looked odd, confused or something. Maybe he just wanted to speak with his friend one-on-one?

Jeremy didn't object. "I'll be back in a few minutes," he promised.

As she went back to her seat, she couldn't help the thoughts that crossed her mind. Was Jeremy going to be like Brad? Was he going to feel she wasn't in the same league as he, and his family and friends, were?

She felt a tightening around her heart.

From the moment Sean called out to him, Jeremy had mixed feelings.

On the one hand, he was really glad to see his friend. They'd spoken on the phone a few times and e-mailed, but it had been about two years since they'd actually gotten together. He'd known Sean was looking to move back closer to home—his parents lived in Staten Island and his wife was from Pennsylvania—but he hadn't heard from him in a while.

On the other hand, he'd been gripped by a fear. Sean had known him for years. Would he say something inadvertently that would reveal info on Jeremy's famous family?

So he'd felt relief when Nicole indicated she'd leave them alone to catch up.

Yet, as she walked back to their seats, he felt a niggling

doubt. Her expression—something in her eyes—bothered him. She'd looked almost suspicious.

"I'm glad to hear you moved closer to me," Jeremy said. "I'd like to get together."

"Yeah, that makes two of us. And with Eric living in Hoboken, we should all get together soon."

"Yeah, we definitely should! How's Samantha?" Jeremy asked. He'd always thought Sean's wife was a nice person.

"She's great." Sean spoke about his wife for a minute, then raised his eyebrows. "So, Jer, who's this gorgeous woman you're with today? Is it a casual date or something more?"

"For sure, it's something more." The words just seemed to pop out of his mouth. As he said them, he realized it was true. Nicole was not a casual date. He really cared for her.

Sean's eyebrows lifted farther. "So, the king of 'I'm going to play the field' is settling down?"

"Whoa," Jeremy said, putting up the hand holding the soda. "I didn't say that. Let's not go too fast, okay?"

Sean laughed. "Okay, so why don't you tell me about her?"

As Jeremy described Nicole's good qualities—her friendliness and warmth, her enthusiasm, not to mention her unbelievable cooking talent—it emphasized what his subconscious mind had been thinking.

Nicole was a fantastic person.

Sean switched to asking about his family—something Jeremy had expected, since Sean was a personable guy—and they filled each other in on how their family members were doing. Jeremy thought again that he was lucky that Nicole had tactfully left them alone and he didn't have to worry about what was said.

"I'm here with my cousin," Sean said after a few minutes. "I'd better get back."

"Yeah, and it looks like the Giants have a chance at another touchdown," Jeremy said, pointing to the TV monitor nearby.

They agreed to talk during the week and make plans to get together. Jeremy turned and started back.

A few yards later, his path was blocked by Brooke.

"What's going on, bro?" she asked. She wore a quizzical expression.

"Nothing," Jeremy said.

"Uh-uh, sorry, but that answer is not going to fly with me. Nicole looked funny when she returned to her seat. I asked her where you were, and all she would say was that you bumped into an old friend."

"It's true," he said defensively. "I saw Sean O'Leary. Remember him?"

Brooke nodded. Sean had been to their house a few times, and Jeremy knew Brooke had met him.

"So, why did Nicole hurry back to her seat looking so . . . pensive?" Brooke asked.

Jeremy shrugged. "I guess she knew I wanted to speak to him for a few minutes."

Brooke frowned. "Did you act like you didn't want her around?"

Jeremy started to protest, but his sister cut in. "Never mind. She probably picked up on the fact that you wanted to talk to him alone."

Several people jostled by, but he could hear her sigh. "You're going to have to tell her eventually, Jeremy. Maybe you should talk to her before she hears about us from someone else."

"The chances of that are slim," he said.

"You ran into Sean," she pointed out.

"I just need more time," he protested. "I don't want her to find out yet. I want to be sure—real sure—that Nicole likes me for myself."

Brooke made a snorting sound. "Ha, I know that already."

Jeremy couldn't be so sure. He wanted to believe his sister was right. But what if she was wrong? What if Nicole had pieced together enough about his family? Maybe she'd even researched him or something! She'd said that she didn't watch the soaps, but if she read the *National Snoop,* she could have seen articles about his mom there. They usually ran one at least once a year. If nothing was happening with her show, they'd dig into nonexistent dirt. A few years back they'd run an article entitled "Is Super Soap Star's Marriage Over?" because his dad had been in Mexico visiting his sister, who was sick, for a couple of months. Another time there'd been a whole spread about how the show might be cancelled—he hadn't any idea where they'd gotten that idea, but there were photos of all the stars.

No, he needed a little more time. "I'm not quite ready to say anything yet," he reiterated to his sister.

Brooke sighed again, then suddenly gave him a hug. "I know where you're coming from, Jer. But I also can judge people pretty well. I don't think you have to worry."

He really wished he felt as confident as his sister, he thought as they returned to their seats.

"Did you and your friend have a good time catching up?" Nicole asked, her voice ultrapolite.

"Yeah, we did, thanks. It's been a long time since we saw each other in person." He took a good look at Nicole. Her expression seemed guarded. "I'd like for you and me to get together with him and his wife sometime soon," Jeremy said impulsively. He wanted to reassure her—but of just what, he wasn't certain.

It must have been the right thing to say, because she did look more relaxed after that.

A sudden roaring around him alerted him to the fact that the Giants were close to making a touchdown.

He refocused on the game.

Something was bothering Nicole, he could tell, but he was unsure what it was. Was she jealous he'd spent time with his friend? That didn't seem like her. She was pretty confident and didn't seem to be the type to be threatened by his having a male friendship. He couldn't figure out what was bugging her—unless she had somehow sensed his hesitancy when he'd seen Sean.

So he made a real effort to give Nicole a lot of attention for the rest of the game.

The game got more exciting as it went on—the Giants scoring, then the other team, then the Giants again. When the Giants won by three points in the last quarter, the fans were screaming.

"Wow, what a game that was!" Jeremy said as they headed out of the stadium. He grabbed Nicole's hand and held on tight.

"That was the best game I've been to in years!" Scott declared, his voice hoarse from shouting.

Nicole smiled, and Jeremy instantly felt better.

He should tell her. He knew that. He just needed a little more time . . .

Chapter Nine

So tell me about this woman you've been seeing," Troy said as Jeremy slid into a seat in the booth opposite his older brother.

Jeremy raised his eyebrows. "How did you know?"

"Brooke's been talking to Rebecca and me," Troy stated.

Jeremy made a snorting sound. Nothing was secret around here, he thought, taking the menu the server handed him.

"Well?" Troy probed.

Jeremy looked up. His older brother had had an appointment with a well-known soap opera actor in the star's home in Mendham. The man, a co-worker of their mother's, had had a recent heart attack and was semi-retired, and Troy had gone out to speak to him about his taxes. Since Troy was less than a half hour away, Jeremy had been happy to meet him for dinner. Brooke had a rehearsal she didn't want to miss that night because there were some scenery problems, so it was just him and Troy.

Maybe, he thought, his brother could give him some advice.

"Nicole's my neighbor," Jeremy began. "She's warm, and friendly, and gorgeous, and a great cook . . ." He went on to describe how he'd gotten to know Nicole, how she'd asked him to be on her show, and their cooking arrangement.

Troy asked one or two questions, but for the most part he simply listened. "She sounds pretty terrific," Troy finally remarked.

"She is!"

"So, what's the problem?" Troy asked as their sampler of appetizers arrived.

Jeremy sighed. "I just want to be sure she likes me, bro—*me*—for myself, and not for my famous family—which includes you."

"Nah, I'm not famous," Troy denied. "I'm the behind-the-scenes accountant."

"You're pretty well-known for an accountant," Jeremy pointed out, munching on a chicken wing.

Troy shrugged. "I don't think so. But"—he held up his hand—"it doesn't matter. I know how you felt after you found Monica only wanted you for your connections. I don't want to ever see you go through that again."

"Yeah," Jeremy said, "and Rebecca went through almost the same thing." In medical school, a couple of guys had been chasing after Rebecca because they'd wanted an "in" to a successful practice. His oldest sister had caught on pretty quickly and put an end to that. Now she was married—to a doctor in a different field, ophthalmology.

His brother did seem to understand, Jeremy thought. Of course, Troy hadn't experienced the same problem. His wife, also an accountant, came from a wealthy family that owned a chain of baby furniture stores, so it wasn't like she wanted Troy for his fame or fortune—she had her own. She loved Troy for himself.

And that's exactly what Jeremy wanted.

His thoughts skidded to a halt. *Love? Whoa,* he told himself. *Let's not get carried away here. Who said anything about love?*

"I'm glad you understand," he told his brother, who had picked up a mozzarella stick. He went on to describe his running into Sean at the game, and how Nicole had seemed hesitant after that.

"Maybe she's unsure about *your* feelings," Troy pointed out. "Women can get emotional if they think you're not appreciating them."

"I've tried to be considerate," Jeremy responded.

"Maybe you should do something nice—something extra, something out-of-the-ordinary," Troy suggested.

"Like what?" Jeremy asked.

They sat in silence for a moment. Jeremy pondered taking her out to a fancy restaurant, buying her a piece of jewelry—but nothing seemed quite right. He bounced the ideas off his brother, but was rejecting them as soon as the words left his mouth.

"She's really special. I need something special, something . . ." He paused as an idea hit him.

"What?" Troy asked as the server returned with their dinners.

Jeremy stared for a moment at his surf-and-turf special. Then, bending his head, he said to Troy, "I have an idea. Tell me what you think of this."

* * *

Wind buffeted Nicole as she hurried up the sidewalk, juggling her tote bag, purse, and dry cleaning. It was going to rain at any minute. She reached the door and unlocked it, dropped her things on a nearby chair, and shut the door—but not before she glanced at Jeremy's house. His van wasn't in the driveway. She'd spoken to him only briefly on Tuesday, and hadn't heard from him since.

She sighed, kicked off her shoes, and went to put her dry cleaning away. With Marla at work, the house was silent.

Jeremy had been on her mind more than she liked since Sunday. She couldn't figure out his strange behavior when he'd run into his friend. Had he been embarrassed to be seen with her? Was he like Brad, and wanted to stick with upper-class friends? But Brad had wanted to show her off—for her looks. Jeremy didn't seem to want that.

Totally confused, she had wondered if she should see him less often—only, she didn't *want* to stop seeing him. She liked him, had a good time with him, and most importantly, she had the show to consider.

But what if theirs was just a casual relationship to him? Or worse still, what if he was using her like Brad had—even if his motive was home-cooked meals, not making someone else jealous?

She changed to jeans, went back downstairs, and grabbed her tote. She really had to work on grading these papers. It was Thursday, and she and Kathy had decided to skip exercise because they both had lots of homework to correct.

As she settled on a chair and began to go through her students' work, rain began to ping against the window. She glanced outside. The gray day looked bleaker than it had a few minutes ago.

She started on her work, but found herself having trouble

concentrating—all because of one green-eyed, handsome man.

The phone rang. She stared at the number coming up. It was Jeremy's. "Hello?" Her voice sounded eager even to her own ears.

"Hey, Nicole, how are you?" Jeremy said in his warm voice.

"I'm fine. How about you?" she inquired. His voice had her humming inside.

They spoke for a few minutes about their jobs, and then Jeremy said, "Listen. Can you put aside the whole day on Saturday?"

"The whole day?" Nicole asked, puzzled. Why would he want her to put aside the whole day? Did he need a favor? Did he want to show her off to some flashy friends, like Brad had?

"Yeah, I want to take you somewhere." It sounded like he was smiling.

"Where would we go?"

"It's a surprise," he said.

A surprise—well, that didn't tell her anything. "What kind of surprise?" she asked, her voice turning cautious.

"It'll be a good one, I promise. I'd like to take you into New York—to a mystery location."

Maybe the theater? she wondered. "Are we going to see a Broadway show?" She could hear the hopeful note in her voice.

"No. I'm not going to tell you. It's a surprise," he repeated. "But I guarantee you'll like it."

"A guarantee?" she said. "Hmm . . ." This was starting to sound better. She relaxed against the chair. "Well, if you can guarantee I'll enjoy it . . ."

"You will," he said emphatically.

"Then, yes, I can put aside the day. But we'll have to change my making dinner for you." On Friday there was a happy hour party for the teachers in Green Valley. Not wanting to miss it, Nicole had already changed her cooking dinnertime with Jeremy from Friday to Saturday.

"No problem. You can cook for me any day. But this is a special treat—for you."

Something in his warm, husky voice sent shivers up her spine. A treat—for her. It sounded delicious.

"Okay," she agreed, without any more thought. "What should I wear?"

"Dress casual. Jeans," he replied.

When he hung up a few minutes later, she found herself smiling. He was planning a surprise, a treat, *just for her.* Suddenly, the gray afternoon had brightened.

"So what's the latest with your new guy?" Kathy asked as she and Nicole slid into their seats in the restaurant at a table with friends.

It was Friday, and the teachers' association happy hour party was already in full swing. A couple of Nicole's friends who taught at one of the elementary schools had waved her and Kathy over. She didn't get to see her friends from outside of her middle school building often and wanted to catch up.

"We want to hear all about him!" Valerie declared, moving slightly in her seat, revealing her growing stomach. Valerie was expecting her second child. She and her husband were happily married and had a two-year-old daughter, Alexandra, and were also raising his nephew and niece, whose parents had been killed in a car crash years ago. Since having her daughter, she'd been able to change her teaching assignment from third grade to teaching remedial reading part-time. Nicole didn't get to see her that often.

"Yeah, spill," Anne urged. Anne had been a divorced mother of one, who, a few years ago, had married a fellow teacher and, like Valerie, was also very happy.

"The latest is . . . he called me a few nights ago and asked me to put aside the whole day Saturday. He has a surprise for me. He's taking me to New York City but he won't tell me what the surprise is," Nicole finished.

"Aha! Tickets to a show?" Anne guessed.

"Maybe a concert or the ballet?" Kathy mused.

"Or you're going to tour some museums and go out to a really great restaurant?" Valerie exclaimed.

"I don't know. He's keeping it a big secret," Nicole said. "But," she added, "he did say not to dress too fancy."

"Hmm . . . no fancy restaurant," Valerie said as a server came over with quesadilla appetizers.

"Maybe another sports game?" Kathy said, furrowing her brow.

"I don't think he'd keep that a surprise," Nicole said. She bit into the tasty quesadilla. The noise level in the room became louder as more teachers entered.

"What could it be?" Kathy asked.

"I can't wait to find out," Nicole announced.

"What does he look like?" Anne questioned.

"He's really handsome!" Kathy said, reaching for a quesadilla. "I watched the cooking show where he first appeared," Kathy continued, surprising Nicole. She hadn't known her friend had watched. "You should see him."

"He is handsome," Nicole said, feeling her cheeks flush. "He's tall, dark, and handsome, and has these bright green eyes . . ."

"Hi everyone," came voices behind Nicole. She turned

to see Ruby and Abby, two other teachers from the elementary school.

It seemed like everyone had heard about Jeremy's visit to her school. Within a few seconds, Ruby was questioning her too.

"But I'm not sure where our relationship is going," Nicole admitted.

Her statement was met with good-natured laughs and smirks.

"Ha," Anne said.

"I've heard that one before!" declared Ruby, pulling over another chair and plopping down. She, too, was pregnant— with twins. She and her husband James had a three-year-old son as well.

"She sounds like you, Valerie," Abby said, "when you were first going out with Douglas."

"They make a perfect pair on TV," Kathy concluded with a blissful sigh.

"And he sounds considerate—taking you to New York for the day," Valerie remarked.

"Oh, he is very nice," Nicole agreed. "I'm just not sure . . ."

"Hey, guys!" Simone, a music teacher from Nicole's school, joined them. "Did you hear the latest about Ms. McElvey?"

"What?" Nicole asked, anxious to change the subject. Except for Kathy, Marla, and her producer Irene, no one knew Jeremy was an "invented" boyfriend, and she didn't want to share that info just yet.

"She's going to take over as principal when Jones retires in December!" Simone declared.

People began to talk excitedly about the woman's move from elementary school principal to high school principal.

Nicole was grateful. She really didn't want to get into details about her relationship with Jeremy and her fears . . . or her dreams.

She'd dreamed about him last night. In the dream they'd been out on his boat, but they'd been wearing dressy clothes. Jeremy had looked devastating in a black suit, and she'd worn a bright blue dress. They'd been standing in the boat, dancing to music—which really made no sense, but it had been so romantic, and she'd woken feeling his arms around her . . .

"Earth to Nicole," Kathy said in a low voice. "Are you thinking about Jeremy?" Her eyes twinkled.

Nicole snapped back to the present. Glasses clinked around her, people laughed, and someone was playing the piano at the end of the room.

"From what I've heard, McElvey is pretty good," Nicole said, trying to continue the hot topic and deflect attention from herself and her relationships. "I think she'll be an asset to the high school."

"Yeah, I just talked to Matt, the band director at the high school, and he said most of the faculty's pretty happy about it," Simone said.

They continued to discuss the topic for several minutes, until someone brought up the rumor that one of the high school vice principals was dating a new teacher—and suddenly that was the big topic of conversation.

Nicole enjoyed talking to her friends, plus she was able to speak to some other teachers she liked but who taught in different areas of her building. A few people came up to her and asked for cooking advice, which was fun.

"I need some recipes that kids will like but are easy for busy families!" Valerie said as she got ready to leave.

"Me too!" Ruby added.

"I'll get a few together and e-mail them," Nicole promised.

By the time the party wound down and she and Kathy left, it was after seven o'clock.

It was only a fifteen-minute drive home. As she turned onto her street, she noticed Jeremy's house was dark. She wondered what he was doing tonight, since she'd had the faculty party to go to.

When she opened the door she found Marla watching TV.

"How was the happy hour?" Marla asked. A vanilla-scented candle flickered on a table near her.

"Good!" Nicole said, plopping down on the couch beside her sister. "How was your day off?"

"It was relaxing," Marla said. "I lazed around." She pointed to the sweats she was wearing.

Nicole knew that Scott was working today, so Marla hadn't seen him, but that they were both off the next day. "What are you and Scott doing tomorrow?" she asked.

"Nothing as exciting as you, I'm sure," Marla quipped.

"I don't know what we're doing." Nicole lifted her hands.

"Well, you're going into the city. That should be fun," Marla said. "I think Scott and I are going to go car shopping."

Nicole raised her eyebrows.

"We're looking for him, not me," Marla hastily added. "He wants me along to help him."

Her eyebrows stayed up. "Is that so?"

"Yes, it is." Marla was smiling.

"You don't know much about cars," Nicole pointed out.

"I know less than he does. But," Marla added, "I do like his company, so I'm going along. We may go bowling at night."

Wow, this sounded like it was getting serious. "He must like you a lot to take you car shopping," Nicole said.

"Do you think so?" Marla asked, her expression pensive.

"Yes . . . or else it's a cheap form of entertainment," Nicole said with a laugh.

Marla threw a pillow at her, but she was laughing too.

Nicole hopped up. "I'm going to take a shower and get comfortable."

A half hour later she was in her favorite blue flannel pajamas, sitting at her desk and checking e-mails. She was reading a joke her brother sent her when she heard her cell phone pinging.

She picked up the phone to find a text message from Jeremy.

SEE YOU TOMORROW, TEN AM! the message stated.

She got up and peeked out her blinds. Lights were now on at Jeremy's house, and his van was in the driveway.

She sat back down and rapidly texted: I CAN'T WAIT!

She was still stupidly grinning at her cell phone when Marla tapped on her door. "Your show's coming on soon."

"Oh, I'd better set up to record it," Nicole said. She liked to keep copies of her shows. It was interesting to see how it was edited.

It was the second episode with Jeremy. Nicole had to admit it had come out well, and afterward she and Marla discussed how Jeremy's presence had affected the show.

"I think it adds some sparkle to the show," Marla said, "a little humor, and a little romance. It was a great show before, but now it really shines!"

"Really?" Nicole asked. "I was afraid it would detract from the food."

Marla shook her head. "Oh no. It's *A Taste of Romance,* remember? It needed this element of romance."

Nicole wasn't so sure. "It was fine before Jeremy appeared."

"Yes, but it's even better now. And . . . now you're getting your own taste of romance!" Marla said, laughing. "Don't deny it."

"It's true," Nicole whispered. Something twisted inside her. "I just don't know if Jeremy feels the same."

"Are you kidding? The guy's crazy for you," Marla said so vehemently that Nicole stared at her sister.

Was he? Warmth and hope washed over her—especially when she realized how much she *wanted* it to be true.

Nicole scrambled excitedly out of bed when her alarm went off at eight the next morning. A quick peek out the window showed her a sunny Saturday, with a few clouds in the bright blue sky. The weather forecasters had said the weekend would bring some sunny but chilly weather, and wind rattled the windows as she went downstairs.

She brewed coffee and made oatmeal. She thought again about what Jeremy's surprise could be and had no idea which of her guesses, if any, was correct. Whatever the surprise was, she was looking forward to it.

She went upstairs with a second mug of coffee and got dressed. She'd chosen a favorite, flattering red sweater; blue jeans; and her old but comfortable short black boots. Knowing they might have to do some walking around the city, she wanted to be sure she wore something comfortable on her feet.

She spent extra time on her makeup and hair, brushing

her hair till the black locks shone. She spritzed on perfume and added gold hoop earrings, a gold bracelet and a simple gold necklace.

She heard Marla come out of her room a little before ten.

"Have fun today!" Marla told her.

"You too!" she said.

A knock on the front door alerted her that Jeremy was there, a few minutes early. She descended the stairs with her sister, and Marla wandered into the kitchen.

Nicole opened the door.

Jeremy stood there, a boyish, happy expression plastered on his face.

She opened the door, and he said, "Today's the day!"

"Are you going to tell me now?" she asked as he stepped inside.

He grinned mischievously. "Not quite yet," he said.

Nicole groaned. Jeremy pulled her into his arms and buried his face in her hair. "I think you'll like it, though," he said, his voice muffled. His breath sent a little shiver of delight up her spine.

She hugged him back. "I'm sure I will."

Jeremy stepped back. "Better bring a jacket or something. It's windy out there."

Jeremy was wearing a black leather jacket that made him look like a model "bad boy" for a TV series. Underneath, he wore a forest green sweater and black jeans and the old black sneakers he favored.

"Okay," she agreed. "Just give me a minute or two."

She heard Marla say hello to Jeremy as she flew upstairs to get her purse and pick out a jacket. She decided on a short, charcoal-gray knit jacket.

She was ready quickly and hurried back downstairs.

After telling Marla to have a good day, they departed.

"We're going to the train station," Jeremy said, indicating his Jeep. He opened the door. "Hop in. Hope you don't mind, but I didn't want to drive into the city. The traffic is bad, and parking is always a problem."

"I don't mind at all," Nicole said. "I usually take the bus. As you said, parking is a problem. Even if you can find a parking lot with available space, it's so expensive." Secretly, she was pleased. Obviously, Jeremy wasn't so rich that he looked down his nose at public transportation.

It didn't take long to get to the train station. "The train should be here in fifteen minutes," Jeremy said. "After that it will only take about an hour to get into the city."

There were just a few people at the station: a guy who looked like a college student; an elderly woman with a huge purse; and a middle-aged woman with a teenage girl. Nicole and Jeremy sat on a bench by themselves, and he put an arm around her shoulders, pulling her close.

"So, where do you think we're going?" he asked, his eyes gleaming.

"Hmm . . . if you had told me to get a little dressed up, I would have thought a play," Nicole mused. "Are we going to a museum?"

"Nope." He grinned.

"Are we going to a concert—or maybe to a play off-off-Broadway where everyone dresses casual?"

He shook his head.

"New York has so many great restaurants. Maybe we're going to a brand new one?" She heard the hopeful note in her voice.

"No, we're not. But," he added, drawing out the words, "you're close."

"Close?"

"Yes." He bent close and his voice dropped. "It has to do with food."

She looked at him, puzzled. What else would have to do with food? He wasn't taking her to a market of some kind, was he? Maybe he was taking her to a gourmet market? That would be interesting. "Are we going to some kind of gourmet market or expo?" she asked.

He leaned closer. "I'll tell you now."

"Yes?" She could hear the anticipatory note in her voice.

"We're going to be in the audience for today's taping of *Chef vs. Chef*."

She couldn't believe they were going to see *Chef vs. Chef!* "Oh!" she screamed. "Oh, Jeremy!" She threw her arms around him. They were going to see her favorite show!

"Oh, I can't believe it! We're going to *Chef vs. Chef*." She was blathering, she knew, but she couldn't help it. "Oh, Jeremy, thank you! What a wonderful surprise—thank you!" She squeezed him tightly. What a great idea! And how thoughtful he was! He'd gotten them tickets to her favorite cooking show! He was the best.

She was barely conscious of the curious looks the other people waiting for the train were sending their way. She was so excited, she could hardly think.

She gave him a resounding kiss.

It was worth the finagling he'd done to get the tickets, just to witness Nicole's excitement, Jeremy thought, holding her close.

He had never seen her so enthusiastic. Her happiness spilled over as she kept thanking him and exclaiming *"Chef vs. Chef!"*

He heard rumbling. "Here comes the train," he said.

She was practically plastered to him. He didn't mind, but they had to get on board in a moment.

"Oh!" she exclaimed again. She pulled back, her smile wide and beautiful. "Oh, Jeremy, you are the greatest. This is the best surprise I've ever had!"

Hand in hand, they boarded and found a seat together. On a Saturday morning the train was mostly empty, and they had the area to themselves.

"How on earth did you get tickets?" Nicole asked as the train began to move forward, its horn blowing and bells ringing.

"I, uhm, kind of called in a favor," Jeremy said. "Someone who knows my brother well"—*yeah,* he thought, *you could say his mother knew his brother well*—"had some pull, and she got the tickets."

And she'd been able to get the tickets with a couple of calls—although his mom *had* expressed surprise at Jeremy's request. "You never ask for favors like this, Jeremy," his mother had said on the phone. "She must be a very special friend."

"She is," he admitted, but didn't want to say more—not yet.

"I hope we can meet her sometime," his mom had continued.

"Yeah, well, I'll bring her over sometime soon," he'd said hastily. "Mom, you're the best."

His mother had laughed. "Keep thinking that."

Now they sat, and Nicole wondered out loud which of the champion chefs would be part of the day's challenge. Her gorgeous face was so animated, for a moment he wanted to cover it with kisses.

"And it will be so interesting to see how they do things, if the battle is as short as it looks on TV or if it stretches out," she went on excitedly. "And it'll be fascinating to watch what they're doing in the studio—the staging, how they're accomplishing everything . . ."

"These seats aren't the closest," Jeremy warned her.

"I don't care if they're far away! The important thing is that you got them!" she declared, beaming. "I can't believe I'm really going to a taping of *Chef vs. Chef.*"

Jeremy relaxed against the seat of the train. He might as well bask in the glory for a while—the glory of pleasing his girlfriend. *Girlfriend?* his mind questioned. He weighed the word as Nicole chatted on. *Yes,* he thought. *Girlfriend.* It sounded exactly right.

Chapter Ten

Nicole could hardly contain her excitement as they rode the train for the hour into the city. They eventually did speak about other things—the Giants' prospects for the rest of the season; a house addition Jeremy had just been hired to wire; Nicole's after-school cooking club, which actually had fifteen kids signed up—but periodically they went back to talking about the show they were going to see.

Marla texted her about half an hour after they got on the train. WHAT'S THE SURPRISE? her message read.

WE'RE GOING TO SEE CHEF VS. CHEF!!! Nicole texted back. She could just imagine how excited Marla would be for her.

WOW! Marla texted back.

When they arrived in the city, Jeremy told her the theater was a long walk—a couple of long city blocks plus several blocks over. He offered to get a cab.

"No, we can walk," Nicole said. "It's a beautiful day and I don't mind. My boots are comfortable."

It was a gorgeous day. The sun was bright, and few clouds marred the blue expanse of sky. The wind was brisk in the city, though, whistling between tall buildings with surprising strength.

They walked hand in hand, speculating on what the secret ingredient for today's show would be. The chefs came prepared to cook, Nicole knew, with some of their own foods. They were also provided a variety of basic ingredients, and just before the competition started, they were given a "secret food" they had to incorporate into their dishes.

"Maybe it'll be chocolate," she suggested. "They've used that a few times."

They strolled down the street, gazing in store windows. Many were decorated in orange and black with Halloween motifs. They stopped to look at some clocks, then a display of colorful scarves. Jeremy paused by a jewelry store with expensive watches.

"Who would pay a thousand dollars for a watch?" he scoffed.

Nicole smiled, gladdened by his remark.

Beautiful, sparkling diamonds caught Nicole's eye. "Look at those," she said, then felt her face grow warm. The oval-shaped diamonds were engagement rings.

"They're nice." Jeremy moved on to look at some men's rings with onyx stones.

They kept going down the street, their hands still linked. Nicole loved the feeling of her hand nestled in Jeremy's, all warm and sheltered.

A few store windows were displaying Thanksgiving decorations too. One store even had a window with a Christmas display.

"That's early," Jeremy said.

"The mall in Rockaway is totally decorated for Halloween," Nicole said. "But watch, on November first a few Thanksgiving displays will go up, but all the rest will be decorated for Christmas and Hanukkah."

They stopped to get thick, warm pretzels that the vendors sold from their street carts. Nicole took hers plain, but Jeremy slathered on mustard. They chose sodas, and ate as they approached the studio.

They arrived at the studio by noon. They were allowed to stand in the lobby with others. Soon it grew more crowded, and Jeremy put his arm around Nicole, drawing her to him. She caught a whiff of his woodsy aftershave.

"I can't wait to see this!" she said.

His eyes gleamed. "I can tell."

Eventually the inner doors were opened and they were allowed to go down a long gray corridor. They passed a store, which a guide said would still be open after the show. Through the glass windows Nicole spotted T-shirts, caps, and a variety of items that read *Chef vs. Chef.*

"We'll look in there after the show," Jeremy promised.

She decided she'd buy him something as a thank-you and something for herself, so she'd always remember this special day.

Their seats turned out to be higher up in the small theater area—an area that held only about two hundred people, she estimated—but they were near the middle, which was ideal. Large-screen TVs were scattered at different points so that the audience could see close-ups as well as the general action on the kitchen stages.

An announcer repeated a message several times, instructing spectators to take photos now, since none would be allowed during the taping of the show. Nicole and Jeremy took photos of each other with their cell phones, and then she turned to the woman next to her and asked her to get one of the both of them.

The audience was a mix of gender and age. Nicole saw several groups of women, couples ranging in age from younger than her and Jeremy to over seventy, and a number of families.

At last the lights were lowered and the master of ceremonies introduced the chefs who would be competing. One, Chef Imperiale, owned an Italian restaurant in Philadelphia, and the other, Chef Garwood, was a master chef who was known for his Mexican-inspired dishes.

"And now, for our special ingredient-of-the-day," the master of ceremonies intoned.

Nicole strained to see as a tablecloth was lifted from a table in the center. On the big-screen TVs, the cameras focused in as the tablecloth rose.

She knew the TV show included a drum roll, but she didn't hear it right now. She guessed they added that during the editing phase. The master of ceremonies paused and then exclaimed, "Peppers!"

The video cameramen moved closer, and on the big screens Nicole could see close-ups of the colorful peppers: red, green, orange and yellow bell peppers; jalepeño peppers; and a kind of pepper she didn't recognize.

The master chefs and their assistants instantly began selecting peppers, placing them in pans and then racing back to their work stations to start preparing their dishes for the grand tasting.

Nicole watched, fascinated, as Garwood began dicing

red peppers, onions, and celery. One of his assistants was scooping out orange peppers and the other appeared to be slicing pepper rings.

She looked at Imperiale. He was also scooping out peppers. One of his assistants had cut red peppers into strips and was drizzling them with olive oil, then sprinkling salt and pepper on top. She quickly put them into an oven. The other assistant was stirring something on the stove.

There were two "reporters" in the stadium, one moving among the chefs and their assistants, the other standing by a podium. Both were making comments at intervals. The woman by the podium was discussing botanical information on peppers.

Nicole glanced at Jeremy, hoping he was as fascinated as she was by the exciting combination of intriguing foods and master chefs at work. He appeared to be absorbed, but then he turned to her and grinned. Lifting her hand, he squeezed it.

Her heart did a flip and she squeezed back.

Then she turned to watch as Chef Imperiale browned hamburger meat. "See that? He's hollowed out a bunch of peppers. My guess is he's going to stuff them."

"With the meat?" Jeremy asked.

"Yes, and he'll probably add some other ingredients— maybe rice and some chopped-up peppers." Several of the TVs were now showing a close-up of one of Imperiale's assistants, dicing yellow peppers into small bits. His knife went so fast it looked lethal.

She looked at Chef Garwood. He seemed to be making some kind of dough mixture. The reporter on the floor said it appeared to be corn bread. As she watched, Garwood added jalapeño peppers that had been diced into bits moments before.

Delicious, spicy aromas were rising all around them. She smelled garlic and roasted peppers and oregano. She was practically salivating.

Within a few minutes, an array of dishes were being prepared. Imperiale had some kind of fish cooking with a red pepper and vodka sauce; Garwood was working on shrimp with peppers and Creole seasonings. Imperiale's assistants began using pineapples with peppers, coconut, peanuts, and chicken.

"I think that's some kind of Thai dish," Nicole whispered, pointing.

In the meantime, Garwood appeared to be making some kind of red pepper mousse as a dessert presentation. Intrigued, Nicole leaned forward, watching as egg whites were whipped.

Now Imperiale was doing a take on the classic sausage and peppers with some handmade pasta. Nicole made herself a mental note to write down notes later so she could try making it at home.

She was conscious, after a moment, that Jeremy was watching her. Glancing back, she saw he was smiling from ear to ear.

"You're enjoying this, aren't you?" he whispered.

"Yes," she said firmly, leaned over to give him a quick kiss, and added, "totally."

A few minutes later she glanced at him. He was watching one of the big-screen TVs, which was showing a close-up of the multicolored peppers being stir-fried with pieces of chicken.

Happiness shot through her. He was enjoying this too, and she was glad. What good would the surprise have been if he was bored? But remembering he'd liked the show on TV too, she was confident he would enjoy the day almost as much as she would.

A sudden gasp had her looking on the stage again, where a pan was smoking. It wasn't something unusual on the show, but cameras zoomed in to get a close-up shot of flames licking at some vegetables.

The master of ceremonies was calmly announcing that this was not an unusual occurrence here, and as the fire was doused, she could hear the collective sighs.

She felt herself sighing with relief too.

The chefs were working in real time, and as the end of the hour drew near, tension mounted. They ran around faster, cooked harder, snapped orders at their assistants more often, and generally grew more frenzied. Nicole could feel the tension escalate as the last ten-minute countdown began. She wasn't sure if she reached for Jeremy's hand or he reached for hers, but she found herself gripping it tightly.

"This is so exciting!" she murmured.

"Come on, come on," someone behind her was saying. "Start plating the food!"

Jeremy smiled. "Yeah, you're right, it is. This feels kind of like a sporting event."

Nicole made a face at him, but she knew he was just teasing. He was having a good time too.

The chefs and their assistants began placing the food artfully on plates. The frenzy increased. Nicole found herself rooting for the visiting chef, Imperiale, although she knew the master chefs usually won. Imperiale was finishing what looked like a sweet pepper cobbler for dessert, while Garwood was plating his green pepper soup.

Nicole relied on the big-screen TVs to see what the dishes looked like close-up. When the final buzzer sounded, she felt some relief—they'd all managed to finish! But she felt sadness too. The most exciting part of the competition was over.

There was a ten-minute break, and then the chefs served the judges their dishes, explaining what they'd cooked and what ingredients had gone into each. Nicole listened intently.

The judges took a few minutes to score the entries. And then the master of ceremonies bowed to each contestant and said, "And the winner is—"

All the members of the audience leaned forward, holding their breaths.

"It's a tie!"

The audience burst out clapping, stomping feet, and whistling. Nicole shrieked.

"What has happened today has happened in our Kitchen Arena only twice before," the master of ceremonies continued when the noise died down. "Congratulations, Chef Imperiale, Master Chef Garwood." He bowed to each one, and they in turn hugged each other.

The master of ceremonies turned to the audience. "And thank you for joining us today."

Lights in the seating area came on, and people began exiting. Nicole stood up reluctantly.

"This was wonderful!" she said, and impulsively hugged Jeremy. "Thank you. I didn't want it to end." She was sorry to go. She could easily have sat through three more competitions.

He hugged her back. "Glad you liked it." He looked pleased.

"Don't forget to visit our store," one of the ushers said cheerfully as they passed.

"Oh, let's take a look," Nicole said.

They spent some time wandering around the large store. Nicole told Jeremy she was getting him something, and he agreed, but only if she let him get her something.

"Pick a few things," Jeremy urged her. "It's your day."

He didn't have to repeat the offer. They strolled through the store, examining items, comparing some things.

She chose a *Chef vs. Chef* T-shirt, and added a spoon rest and coffee mug with the show's logo. She was interested in a couple of cookbooks, but decided to order them from the Web site. She didn't want to ask him to spend a lot of money on her. He'd already gone out of his way enough!

Jeremy selected a *Chef vs. Chef* cap and a travel coffee mug for his van.

Once they paid for each other's items, they walked back to the street.

It was about four-thirty. The day had grown cooler, with the wind picking up considerably, gusting every few minutes. Clouds now covered the sky.

But Nicole was so happy, the weather was still beautiful to her.

"Want to eat dinner around here?" Jeremy asked.

"I'd love to—although it is kind of early," she replied.

"Yeah, but we didn't have lunch, except for the pretzels." He patted his stomach. "I'm hungry, especially after smelling all that good food. How about we walk around and see if we spot a place that looks good?"

"Okay," she agreed.

She stopped to look back at the studio. The marquee read *Chef vs. Chef this Saturday!*

Then she looked at Jeremy.

He was smiling at her. He looked boyish and appealing and happy.

And that's when she knew: she was in love with him!

Chapter Eleven

The heady feeling of love filled her, like sweet iced tea being poured from a pitcher, sliding into her entire being. It traveled from the top of her head to her toes, smooth and delicious.

She was in love with Jeremy Perez!

He was so caring, thoughtful, fun to be with, intelligent, and had a good sense of humor—she couldn't begin to list all his good qualities.

She firmly pushed aside the doubts about his background and status. She'd consider that topic another day. Those negative thoughts could stay in the back of the pantry in her mind.

Today was about reveling in his company, enjoying every moment, celebrating the day and the fact that she was in love with this very special man.

"Thank you, Jeremy!" she exclaimed, and throwing her arms around him, kissed him right there on the busy New York street. She could feel the sparks of love and attraction cascade right through her.

Jeremy kissed her back, hard, holding her tightly.

When she finally pulled back, she felt almost dizzy, her entire self as warm as the kitchen stoves she'd watched, overflowing with love instead of food.

Jeremy was smiling down at her. "I'm glad you liked it," he said.

She hugged him. "This was one of the best days of my life."

"And it's not over," he said.

People walked around them, some ignoring them, others smiling good-naturedly. Jeremy took her arm and began steering her down the street. "Let's find somewhere to eat."

They fell into step together, arms around each other.

Nothing could hide the spring in her step or, she was sure, the blissful smile on her face. *She loved Jeremy!*

Jeremy held onto Nicole as they walked up the city street, holding the bag with their purchases. Wind cooled his heated cheeks but didn't dampen his enthusiasm.

Wow, that had been some kiss.

Nicole had been practically dancing on air all day, but this latest kiss had him feeling as if a mega-jolt of electrical current had just zapped him. Every cell in his body was alive, bright, and totally aware of Nicole and his surroundings.

Had he ever made anyone so happy? Well, maybe his mom and dad with his childish drawings and performances on his drums, or maybe the first time he'd been on his mom's show with his brother and sisters, or when he graduated from college with honors—maybe those things had made his parents happy, but they paled in comparison with this. Nicole had worn a thrilled expression on her face all day, since he'd first told her about the show, but now she positively radiated joy.

He hoped it wasn't just the show. He hoped—actually, he was pretty certain—it was also because she was with him.

They walked along, and he couldn't help grinning in response to her glowing face.

They crossed a street. *Uh-oh,* he thought. Just ahead was an Italian restaurant that was a favorite of his mom's. His family frequently ate there, and someone was sure to recognize him.

Nicole pointed to it. "There's a place. I've heard of Tortorelli's."

"Your Italian food is so good, I don't think any restaurant can compare," he improvised. "How about trying something else?" He thought about the dishes they'd seen prepared. "How about Thai food? That chicken dish with the peppers and pineapple looked really good."

"Okay," Nicole agreed.

They passed a steak house and a Spanish restaurant before coming to a street overflowing with different places to eat. In the middle of the block was a Thai restaurant. Jeremy had never eaten there, so it was as new to him as it was to Nicole, a safe place to eat where he could be inconspicuous.

Since it was early, the restaurant was almost empty. They were shown to a table at once.

He gazed at Nicole as she studied her menu. She was truly gorgeous, but her enthusiasm and happiness brought a special beauty to her face.

Her eyes met his, and her mouth lifted in that fantastic smile of hers.

He was one lucky guy, he thought, to be out with this woman, and to know that one-of-a-kind smile was just for him.

"What are you going to order?" she asked.

He'd barely glanced at the menu.

"Hmm . . . let me see." He studied the menu and finally selected a chicken dish with pineapples that sounded like what the chef had been cooking.

The lighting in the restaurant was low, making it feel cozy. After they gave their orders, Jeremy snagged Nicole's hand and brushed his thumb across it.

Her hand was soft and feminine. He loved holding it, and it fit perfectly in his.

She smiled at him. "Tell me what you thought of the show," she prompted.

For the next fifteen minutes they discussed what they'd seen and heard and smelled in the Cuisine Arena, as the announcer called the studio. Nicole explained a little about some of the food being prepared, things he hadn't been aware of.

When their food arrived, he dug in. The food was spicy and good, but nothing compared to Nicole's home cooking, and he told her so.

She flashed him her usual big smile. "Thank you." She speared a piece of her peanut chicken. "Want to taste this?"

He took the offered chicken and had a bite. "It's good, but I stand by what I said. Nothing is as good as your food."

She laughed, and the sound flowed over him like warm honey.

Their dinner was relaxing, and they finished with tea.

It was almost dark outside when they left the restaurant. Of course the neon city lights glimmered all over, making the streets almost as light as day. Jeremy pulled Nicole close, tucking her against him, and they walked back to the train station, the wind at their backs now, as they chatted and laughed.

They had almost a thirty-minute wait till their train arrived, and they wandered around the station for a few minutes, arms wrapped around each other, and then sat on a bench. Jeremy pulled her to him and rested his chin against her silky hair, breathing in the fruity scent of her shampoo. Holding each other close, they were warm and cozy. Despite the bright lights and bustle of people coming and going, they had a quiet little space all to themselves.

Jeremy snuggled closer, unbelievably content. He could stay like this, cuddled with Nicole, for hours and hours and be perfectly happy.

She must have been just as content because for several minutes she didn't speak, either. They simply sat together, and Jeremy kept thinking what a great place the world was. How could he not believe that when he held Nicole like this? Her sunny disposition, her warmth—the world really was a better place when he was with her.

He brushed a kiss across the top of her head, and she tightened her hand in his.

An announcer came on the speaker, rattling off the list of trains soon departing. A few minutes later, she announced the arrival of theirs.

"We should go," Nicole said. He heard the note of reluctance in her voice.

"I guess so—although I could stay like this for hours," he admitted.

Nicole smiled at his words, and straightened up. "Come on."

Once on board, they slid into a bench seat and once again cuddled close. As the train pulled out of the city, Jeremy thought he couldn't remember a day that had ever been so much fun. "This was a wonderful day," he told her, stroking her hand with his thumb.

"I agree. I had the best time," she murmured, snuggling still closer.

As the train moved out of the city, and the bright lights gradually gave way to darker patches, they sat quietly together. He almost didn't want to talk, or do anything to break the enchantment that seemed woven around them. Peace, happiness, and an intense awareness of the woman beside him encompassed his soul.

Nicole said little, seeming to be as content as he was to simply just be together.

It wasn't till they arrived and got into his car, where he switched on the music from his iPod, that they began to talk.

"I'm so glad you were delighted with the show and all the food preparations," Nicole said, "and that I wasn't the only one enjoying it!"

The music of an old Beatles song flowed through the air. "I really liked it," Jeremy said, "more than watching it on TV. I knew cooking was part science—measuring and getting things right—but now I think it's an art form too. That's from watching you," he added. "Since you started cooking for me and I watch you on the show, I really appreciate the art of cooking. And watching *Chef vs. Chef* was more exciting than it would have been a few months ago."

"You didn't really see much cooking at your house, did you?" Nicole asked as he pulled onto the main road. Wind shook the car slightly.

"No." He sighed. "But my parents were good in a lot of other ways. They always spent a lot of time with us doing things—even if it wasn't cooking."

"Did you eat a lot of macaroni and cheese?" Nicole asked lightly.

He shook his head. "We didn't any more than other American kids, I guess. We did have a housekeeper when I was young . . ." It slipped out of his mouth without thought. He hadn't meant to say anything about his family's situation! Wondering if she would question him, he rushed on, hoping she wouldn't make too much of his statement. "We were all close in age, and my mom needed help, and Mrs. Turner was nice, but she cooked very simple, basic meals. Turkey and mashed potatoes and green beans were typical."

Nicole made a sympathetic sound.

He slowed at a red light and turned to her, his heart beating faster. He hoped she wouldn't pursue his mention of the housekeeper and what it implied. He wanted, needed, to have this time with Nicole last a little longer, this time where he didn't have to worry about revealing his background.

He wanted it for a few more days, just a few more. He almost whispered the words out loud.

He deflected the conversation. "I guess you watched your mother cook often?"

"And my grandmother—I still ask her questions and get tips from her."

"I'll bet they can't cook as well as you."

She laughed quietly. "I appreciate the thought, but I'm not sure that's true."

"It is." He reached over and grasped her hand, then let go and signaled a right turn.

"Did you ever have homemade mac and cheese?" she asked.

"Uh-uh," he said as he shook his head, "we never did."

"I'll have to put that on the list of dishes to show you," she mused.

"It's gonna be a long list," he warned, chuckling.

Their conversation continued in a light vein until they reached their street. Nicole invited him in to have his favorite brownies. She'd made them several days before and froze them, she said.

Lights were on in her house, and they discovered Marla and Scott were there, back from car shopping, eating, and bowling. They shared the brownies and spoke about their days. Scott was pretty sure which car he was going to pick, and Nicole and Jeremy described the show they'd seen.

"Too bad they don't let you sample the food," Jeremy said, helping himself to another brownie.

"It was wonderful just the way it was," Nicole said, stirring her hot cocoa.

He'd had such high energy all day, but now that it was winding down, he felt tired but satisfied. They watched *Chef vs. Chef* with her sister and Scott. But at midnight, when it ended, he found he'd run out of steam.

"Don't forget we're going to make dinner together tomorrow," Nicole reminded him as he prepared to leave.

"I won't." He was running over to visit his parents in the early afternoon, but he wasn't staying long. He knew they'd welcome Nicole, but that would have to wait till after he revealed all to her. "I'll be here by five."

He pulled her into his arms and gave her a resounding kiss, a kiss that reverberated through his whole self. "See you tomorrow," he said, his forehead touching hers.

She smiled softly. "See you tomorrow," she replied.

"So when are we going to meet this girlfriend of yours?" Rebecca asked, easing into a chair near Jeremy.

Jeremy raised his eyebrows. "You think I have a girlfriend?"

"Come on, I've already talked to Brooke. She said you're crazy about some girl named Nicole."

"Yeah, so, I'm crazy, huh?" Jeremy couldn't help grinning. "Well . . . maybe I am. I'm crazy about her cooking anyway," he added. But he knew that wasn't all.

"Stop teasing." Rebecca frowned. "I'm pregnant and I don't have the patience for it."

"Okay, you'll have the baby soon and then I can go back to it," Jeremy said.

His sister threw a pillow at him. "Don't even think about it."

He laughed. It was good to hang out here, with his family. Troy and his wife were playing with their daughter and his dad in the family room. Rebecca's husband was talking in the kitchen with their mom and Brooke and Will.

He'd been surprised when Brooke had brought Will over, but then he realized he shouldn't have been. Will had known everyone in the family for years.

"You're not staying for dinner?" Rebecca asked.

He shook his head. "Actually, Nicole's teaching me to cook something."

"You . . . cook?" Rebecca rolled her eyes. "Miracles do happen."

Jeremy explained about Nicole's show. When Rebecca questioned him further, he admitted to his big sister that Nicole didn't know anything about his family "except that we're well-to-do. And that's the way I want it to stay," he said firmly, "at least for now."

Rebecca, he knew, would understand. Not only did she know about his old girlfriend, but years ago two guys had run after her, hoping they'd be able to marry her and step into their father's medical practice. When Rebecca had found out that both were bragging to friends that each one "had it made," that had been the end of those relationships. It wasn't until several years later, when she'd met her husband, a doctor specializing in ophthalmology, that she'd finally begun to trust men again. She and her husband had been married for several years now and were expecting their first baby in a couple of months.

His sister gave him a sympathetic look.

"Okay, I can respect that."

Brooke had entered the room. "You still didn't tell Nicole, did you?" she accused him.

"No—but I will," he added.

She exchanged an unreadable look with Rebecca. Turning back to him, she said, "Don't wait too long. What if she finds out before you tell her?"

"She won't," he said confidently.

"But what if she did?" Rebecca asked, shifting in her chair.

His sisters were starting to annoy him. "I'll deal with it. She's a nice, reasonable person. She won't get too upset."

"Hmph," Brooke commented.

"I don't understand men," Rebecca grumbled.

A prickle—just the smallest touch—of fear jarred him.

She wouldn't get really upset, would she?

Nicole was a happy, easygoing person. She wasn't a high-strung type or someone prone to temper tantrums. She wouldn't blow up.

At least, he didn't think so.

Maybe he should talk to her soon—but not today.

Tuesday afternoon, Nicole pulled into the driveway and made a dash for the house. Even though she held an umbrella, cold rain hit her.

Kathy was fighting off a cold and Nicole had decided that instead of exercising alone, she would go straight home. It was a perfect day for a hot bowl of soup, she thought as she entered the house, and curling up with a good book. Not that her mood matched the gloomy day—it was the opposite. She had felt great since Saturday.

She'd spent Sunday evening with Jeremy, teaching him how to make a simple corn bread and her favorite no-bean chili. She'd even divulged her secret to making chili the Mexican way: adding a small amount of chocolate. They'd watched a movie afterwards, cuddled close on the couch.

She hadn't seen him yesterday, but he'd called and they'd talked for a while. And the glow she always felt when she heard his voice, or saw him, stuck with her.

She was totally in love, and it felt good.

Of course, she wasn't sure he felt the same, but she hoped he was falling for her too. She was pretty certain he felt affection for her—which could, hopefully, lead to something more. It just seemed to have happened a lot faster for her than for him.

She got into comfortable sweats and started making some minestrone soup, then sat down with a book. Marla was at work, and she knew Jeremy saw his sister Brooke on Tuesdays, so she had a nice quiet evening to herself.

She read for a while, finished the soup, and then had some while watching the news. She checked her e-mail and sat down on the couch to read again. The rain pinged rhythmically against the window.

All the while, Jeremy was at the back—and front—of her mind. It was as if his image were imprinted there.

She heard the train whistle faintly from the tracks that ran through the northern end of town. She closed her eyes, thinking about the train rides they'd shared into and out of the city, and she couldn't help but smile as she recalled being ensconced in Jeremy's arms . . .

She was in a church. Was Marla getting married? She looked closer, and saw that her sister was wearing a pink gown with a matching jacket. She must be a bridesmaid. And . . . was that Brooke in a matching dress?

She glanced down and realized she was the bride.

She was marrying Jeremy? She smiled as she heard organ music . . .

A car door slammed nearby, startling her awake.

She had dozed off, even with the light on. Someone had gotten in or out of a car nearby, and the sound had woken her.

Rain was now beating harder against the windows. She got up to close the curtain and couldn't help looking at Jeremy's house.

There were lights on in the house now. It must have been his car door that she heard.

She felt like a love-struck teenager, guilty of watching the home where her boyfriend lived. She quickly closed the curtains.

Her dream, though, stayed with her. Being married to Jeremy . . . the idea was really, really appealing.

Somehow, in the last few days, she had pushed aside her fears that Jeremy was a rich guy who was using her, her fears that he was only interested in a superficial relationship. Jeremy wasn't like that. He was a nice guy, and he seemed to genuinely like her.

She trusted him, and it was a good feeling.

Jeremy pounded up the stairs, thinking about his dinner with his sister.

Brooke had berated him, telling him again that he should stop keeping his background a secret from Nicole and tell her the truth about their family.

He'd made no promises—just told his sister he'd think about it.

He went to the front window of the room upstairs that he used as his office. Moving the blinds slightly, he peered out.

The light was still on downstairs in Nicole's house, although now the curtains were drawn.

He sighed. He was too old to be acting like a moonstruck teen!

But he stayed where he was, staring at her house, wondering what she was doing now, this very minute.

It wasn't too late—only nine o'clock. He could call her. And tell her . . . ?

No, he wanted, he needed, just a little more time. Memories of Monica still niggled at the edges of his mind.

Although, come to think of it, he could barely remember what she looked like. He probed, and the sore spot finally produced a hazy picture of his old girlfriend. But like an old photo, it seemed fuzzy and stained at the edges.

He shrugged. It was better that he couldn't remember Monica too clearly.

He kicked thoughts of his old girlfriend out the door of his mind, and sat down in an old, comfy chair to call Nicole—just to tell her he was thinking of her . . . nothing else, for now.

"Hey, Nicole."

Nicole looked at her sister as she dropped her bag and purse on a table, then shut the front door on Wednesday after work. Marla sounded and looked lethargic. She sat on the couch in jeans and an old blue sweater, her feet encased in old gray socks, her face devoid of its usual perky expression.

"Are you okay? Are you sick?" Nicole asked anxiously. Marla rarely got sick, but she didn't look too good. Had something happened to one of the premature babies on Marla's ward last night? The staff worked hard to save them, but some of the preemies were so tiny, and not all of them survived. Just a few months ago they'd lost two within one week, and Marla had been very upset.

"I'm fine." But her sister didn't sound fine. She sounded disheartened.

Nicole plopped down beside her. "Okay, Marl, tell me what's wrong."

For a moment Marla looked straight ahead; then she shrugged. "Scott and I had an argument."

"Oh." Nicole hesitated, unsure what to say next. She moved closer and put her arm around her sister. "How about I make some cocoa and we can talk about it?"

"Okay," Marla agreed.

Nicole hurried into the kitchen and made instant cocoa for them both—this was no time to start making it from scratch. Once she returned to the living room with two mugs and sat beside her younger sister, they both put their feet up on the old coffee table. Marla bent her head, blew on the hot cocoa, and then took a cautious sip.

Nicole watched, sipping her own cocoa. "So, what happened?"

Marla sighed and focused on Nicole. "It wasn't a big fight, actually. I just feel bad about it."

"What did you fight about?"

She shook her head. "I'd rather not say."

"Okay." Nicole didn't want to infringe on her sister's

privacy, but she was curious. "He wasn't mean or anything when you fought, was he?"

"Oh, no." Marla shook her head. "He was actually polite, even when we argued. He just—let's just say he disagreed with something I did. And now I'm wondering if he's right."

"Is it something at work?" Nicole asked.

"No."

"Well, I'm sure you're right," Nicole said loyally.

Marla regarded her. "I'm really not sure." She sipped her drink, her eyes serious. "He made a pretty good argument for his case, explaining why he thinks I should have acted differently. I didn't agree, and told him it wasn't his business." She sighed. "But now, when I think about it, I'm wondering—is his way of looking at the situation correct?"

"I'm sure whatever it is, you know what you're doing," Nicole said staunchly. She wondered again what her sister had done that she now was feeling confusion about. Usually they shared stuff like this. Why wouldn't Marla tell her? Maybe she had promised someone to keep a secret.

"I just don't know," Marla repeated.

"Well, why don't you think about it for a day or two?" Nicole suggested. "Maybe you'll see both sides of the argument more clearly then, and can decide if you're right, or if you should rethink Scott's ideas."

"That's a good suggestion," Marla said, sounding more positive.

Nicole put down her mug and gave her a hug. "You can always talk to me."

"I know. Thanks, Nic."

"Now," Nicole said, pulling back and studying her sister's face, which did have more color in it, "how about we go exercise together and then go out for a bite to eat?"

"Okay," Marla agreed. "Wait—even better, why don't we eat at the mall and do some shopping?"

They exercised, showered, and drove to the mall where they had salads and then spent an hour shopping. Nicole found a rose-colored top that she loved, and Marla bought the same one in sapphire blue. Marla also found short stylish boots and Nicole got a practical pair of black shoes for teaching.

It was almost nine o'clock when they returned home, and she was glad they'd gone out. Marla looked happier, and Nicole was sure her problem would work itself out.

"Thanks," Marla said as they entered the house. She gave Nicole a swift hug. "I feel better."

"I'm glad," Nicole said.

She put away her purchases, thinking about wearing the top on Friday for her TV show. She heard Marla get on her phone, and then went to check her e-mail.

Jeremy, as usual, had been on and off her mind all day. He'd called last night just to say hi, which had been sweet. She wondered if she should do the same.

Impulsively she picked up her cell phone and left the computer, punching in his phone number.

He picked up on the first ring. "Hello?"

They talked for a while, agreeing to meet Friday afternoon and drive together to the TV studio.

Nicole smiled as she clicked her phone shut twenty minutes later.

He was wonderful!

Jeremy was glad he'd cooked with Nicole over the weekend. Cooking on TV, even with a rehearsal, wasn't easy. It was more difficult than simply appearing on camera and smiling and saying a few lines about how great the meal she'd prepared was.

The cameras zoomed in as he cut onions and stirred a corn bread mix. Even with Nicole's guidance, he felt a little self-conscious. Cooking didn't come naturally to him.

Nicole, on the other hand, looked terrific in a silky short-sleeved dark pink top and black pants. She was enthusiastic but calm as they taped the show.

He felt relieved, though, as the show wound down to the closing.

"That wasn't so difficult, was it?" Nicole asked him as the cameras moved closer.

They'd already rehearsed this part. "No," he said slowly, "and it was fun." That part, at least, was true. Anything was fun with Nicole—especially kissing her. He thrust the thought aside for later, putting his arm around her shoulder and squeezing her close to his side. "We'll cook together again."

Nicole beamed, first at him, then the cameras. "Yes, we will! Watch for our next show, when Jeremy will be assisting me again!"

A few seconds went by, then Shelley called "Cut!"

He felt his body sag as the tension left it.

"That wasn't so bad, was it?" Nicole asked.

"Well . . . ," he teased, looking at her face.

Instant concern appeared there. He laughed, and she frowned.

"You're teasing," she accused him.

"Yeah." He hugged her. "You're right, it wasn't bad. I was afraid I'd mess up."

"You did fine," she reassured him. "And you're not usually worried about being on TV."

"No." He skirted that topic. "How about I help you pack up and we go back to my place and relax?"

She smiled. "Okay."

An hour later they were ensconced in front of his TV, eating some popcorn and watching a basketball game.

The coach for the New York team called a time-out, and an advertisement for a restaurant chain came on.

"Your cooking is so much better than theirs," Jeremy said, playing with Nicole's silky hair.

"You think so?" She regarded him.

"I know so." He brushed his lips against hers.

She smiled, but seemed to be studying him.

"Listen," Jeremy murmured, "I want to do something special for you. You always make me the best meals, but how about if we go out tomorrow to a nice restaurant? Cooking is hard work, and I'm obviously not very good at it. I'll take you out for dinner."

"You're getting better at cooking!" Nicole praised, leaning into his embrace.

"Someday I'll cook for you," he said. He nuzzled her hair with his chin. "But that's for another time."

"You cooking for me? I really would like that." She grinned up at him.

"I will," he promised.

"That would be wonderful," she said.

Later, after he walked her home, Jeremy got ready to sleep, feeling happy and content.

He was lucky. His girlfriend was great—his girlfriend, Nicole.

As he drew up the covers, something pricked at his consciousness. What? he wondered.

He felt close to Nicole—close enough to think of her as

his girlfriend, close enough to offer to cook for her some-day . . .

And then he remembered. He hadn't said anything yet to Nicole about his family.

And he should. If they were boyfriend and girlfriend, then she had the right to know about his background and the potential limelight in which she could find herself.

For the last few years, he had managed to fly under the radar. But as Brooke had reminded him only a few nights ago, it was only fair to warn Nicole what she might run into when she was with him. And they'd probably be spending more and more time together.

He'd wanted more time before he told her. He'd needed it. And he'd gotten exactly that.

He suspected that she cared about him—a lot. It seemed he'd finally found a woman who cared about him, for his own sake. It had nothing to do with his family.

He had to tell her.

Okay, he'd tell her tomorrow.

Saturday afternoon, Nicole was sitting on the couch with Marla, chatting. They'd just made two peach cobblers—one for her and Jeremy to share after dinner, and one for Marla and Scott—plus brownies for the local soup kitchen, which they'd frozen till Nicole could deliver them on Monday.

She'd confided in Marla about how she'd fallen in love with Jeremy.

"I knew it!" Marla said. "I knew you were falling in love. And I think Jeremy's falling in love with you!"

"I hope so," Nicole said, her voice wistful. "So . . . tell me about you and Scott. Did you make up from your fight?"

Marla blushed. "Yes . . . ," she said slowly. "We kind of agreed to disagree, and yes, we made up, but . . ."

A car door slammed outside.

"Nic, there's something I wanted to tell you . . ." Marla began.

The doorbell interrupted her.

Nicole glanced out the window. "It's Kathy."

She hadn't expected her, but she hopped off the couch and went to let her in.

"Hi!" she said.

Kathy appeared flustered. Her jacket was open, and she was wearing jeans and a faded sweatshirt. Her usually cheerful expression had changed to one of concern.

"Come on in," Nicole said, wondering what was wrong. "What's up?" She closed the door behind her friend.

"Nicole, have you seen this?" Kathy asked. She dropped her purse on the floor and held out a paper.

It was one of those tabloids.

"The *National Snoop?*" Nicole asked. "I don't usually read that, except to look at the headlines when I'm on line at the supermarket."

"I was there, picking up a few things when I saw this," Kathy said.

Marla had come to stand behind Nicole.

"What's in it?" Nicole was curious, but she had also caught Kathy's anxiety, and her stomach tightened. What could it be?

With a dramatic flourish, Kathy opened the paper to the center.

Nicole stared at the fuzzy photo of herself with Jeremy on her cooking show.

Chapter Twelve

The headlines under the photo read "TV Star's Son Launching His Own Career?"

"*What?*" she gasped. What were she and Jeremy doing in the *National Snoop?* And what the heck did they mean, "TV star's son"? What TV star did they mean? What son were they talking about? Confused, Nicole grabbed the newspaper and stared at the printed page.

The unclear photo was of her and Jeremy, on her show, a couple of weeks before. They were both smiling, and Jeremy had a fork halfway to his mouth.

She read out loud to her sister and friend: "It appears that Jeremy Perez, son of America's darling soap star Sharon Maloney-Perez, is considering his own career in TV. He's been featured recently on *A Taste of Romance,* a cooking show on local cable TV station WKMC in Morris County, NJ."

Ice filled her veins as she continued reading: "Astute viewers who keep tabs on *All My Relatives* know that Sharon Maloney-Perez married Dr. Antonio Perez many years ago in a whirlwind romance. Since then, they have raised four children, two boys and two girls. All four of their children have appeared periodically on *Relatives,* as well as starring in high school, camp, and college productions. Although daughter Brooke Perez does scenery design and teaches theater arts classes at Quemby College in western New Jersey, none of the Perez children seemed destined to go into acting—that is, until now.

"*National Snoop* caught sight of Jeremy Perez on this local cooking show, and has learned that it's likely this is only the beginning of his foray into the world of television. Rumors are he's thinking of joining the cast of *All My Relatives* in the spring."

As she read each word, Nicole's heart grew leaden, until she felt like it was sinking into the floor, disappearing beneath the floorboards, into the depths of the earth.

Jeremy was the son of a famous TV star! No wonder he shied away from talking about his family. And he'd been using her to get back into the world of television?

"This can't be—this is—I can't believe it," she sputtered. "How could he keep it a secret that his family's so famous?" She stared at the caption under the photo. She finished reading: "Jeremy Perez now has a role as leading man with local chef Nicole Vitarelli on her cooking show. Is it real, or is this a romance cooked up for TV?"

But she *could* believe it. Sudden tears sprang to her eyes. "Oh, no," she whispered, "how could he have fooled me like that? He's—oh, *no*—he's just like Brad!" She felt as if her insides were being squeezed, like an orange.

Was it still just a romance cooked up for TV? It had started that way—but, for her, it had become so much more.

She raised her eyes and looked at Kathy, who was in front of her. Her friend wore a look of total sympathy.

Nicole turned to look at Marla, who had reached out to grip her shoulder.

Marla looked . . . funny, and almost . . . almost—Nicole's mouth opened wide—almost . . . *guilty.*

"Marla?" Nicole asked, shock reaching through the pain inside her. "You—you knew about this?"

Tears came into Marla's eyes. She nodded slowly.

"How—how could you . . . ?" Nicole was at a loss.

"Sit down." Marla steered her to the couch and dropped down beside her. Kathy took a seat on the chair near them. "I was just about to tell you."

Something between a sob and a laugh came out of Nicole's throat. "How long?" she choked out.

"I've known for a few weeks." Marla looked rather miserable now.

"How—"

"I watch the soaps, remember? I've followed *All My Relatives* for a while, and I've heard the story of Jeremy's mother. She met his dad when she broke her arm or a finger or something, they had a whirlwind romance, and they've been happily married for over thirty-five years— longer than most TV stars. I was watching one day when I began to put two and two together."

Kathy remained silent.

"Why didn't you tell me?" Nicole's voice came out strained.

Somewhere in her head, she knew that, by focusing on her sister's silence, she could avoid thinking about Jeremy's betrayal, at least for a few minutes.

"Because you were so happy," Marla said, and her voice grew more determined. "You've been so—so quick to distrust men, so unwilling to give anyone a chance. You finally seemed to have found someone you liked, someone you were growing to care for, someone who treated you well! And he seemed to care just as much for you! I didn't want to disrupt that. Can you understand?" Marla sounded a little desperate.

Nicole wasn't sure what to say.

Marla grabbed her hand. "Nicole, I love you. I could see how happy you were, and Jeremy *does* treat you well. I figured he'd tell you eventually, and it was better coming from him."

Nicole swallowed. She could understand her sister's intentions. "You wanted me to establish a relationship with Jeremy before you said anything?"

"Yes! I wanted the bonds between you to grow before I said anything that might disrupt it. It wasn't as if I thought he was like Brad! It was obvious from the start that Jeremy cared for you. He really is a good guy."

"I thought so." It came out harshly. "I guess I was wrong . . ."

"No," Marla protested, "you were right. But I was going to tell you, now, when you said you loved him. I fully expected that you would say you already knew . . ."

"But I didn't," Nicole said, her voice hoarse.

"You had no clue?" This came from Kathy.

"No . . . ," Nicole started, then fell silent.

The clues *had* been there. She just hadn't picked up on them. "I—guess I did," she said slowly. "I was surprised at how comfortable Jeremy was in front of the cameras, and I knew he came from a wealthy area. I just didn't figure out the whole puzzle."

Another thought occurred to her, and she refocused on Marla. "Is this why you fought with Scott?"

"Yes," Marla admitted. "He thought I should tell you right away, and I wanted to hold off."

"I wish you had told me," Nicole said. But as she looked at her sister's stricken face, she knew Marla had only acted in what she thought was her best interest. "But . . . I understand why you didn't, Marl."

"I'm sorry!" Marla exclaimed, and then hugged Nicole tightly. "I'm so sorry. I didn't mean to cause you pain— I just thought I should let things happen naturally and Jeremy should tell you himself—and then I thought maybe he had already told you . . ."

"It's okay," Nicole said, patting her sister.

"Can you forgive me?"

"Yes . . . but I can't forgive Jeremy." She pulled back and regarded Marla.

"I can't believe he's waited this long to tell you," Marla said.

"I can't either!" Kathy declared loyally. "What's his problem?"

"Maybe he never intended to tell me," Nicole choked out. "Maybe . . . maybe this . . . this rag is right. Maybe he cooked up the romance just to get back on TV . . ."

But as she said the words, she found herself shaking her head. "No—I asked him," she contradicted herself.

"Maybe he's just taking advantage of the opportunity?" Kathy guessed.

"Or maybe that stupid paper—it's not even a paper!— is wrong," Marla said hotly.

Nicole stared at the paper. The hole in her soul was still painful. But, slowly, she became conscious of something else: anger. It had been simmering slowly through her, and now it was coming to a boil. How could Jeremy hide this from her? Why hadn't he told her the truth? "He has a lot of nerve, not telling me." Nicole's voice was so harsh it startled even herself. "How could he?"

Marla and Kathy stared.

"He should have," Kathy agreed.

"He never tried?" Marla asked, biting her lip.

"No, he didn't." That anger was growing inside her, and she felt like a sauce that was starting to bubble and pop. "No, and he should have told me the truth! At least . . . at least Brad never hid the fact that he was rich and had connections. I'm going to give Jeremy a piece of my mind when he gets back!" She knew his van had left sometime that morning; she was going to march over there when he returned.

"I think you're going to get your chance soon," Marla said, glancing warily at the window. "I think I just heard his truck pull in."

"Can I have the paper?" Nicole asked Kathy.

"Of course you may." Kathy looked a little scared, and Nicole guessed that her face must look as thunderous as she was feeling. "I guess I'd better get going—I have groceries in the car," she added.

"Thanks," Nicole said hastily.

She didn't even stop to put on her coat. She opened the door and stepped outside. As she did, she heard her cell phone ringing in the house.

It would have to wait.

She marched across the street, the cool wind feeling good against her heated face. She ran up the few steps to Jeremy's front door and rapped on it loudly.

The door opened immediately. Jeremy stood there, his cell phone against his ear.

He broke into a smile. "Nicole, I was just calling you! How are you?"

He looked, unfortunately, as handsome as ever, and

his face was warm and welcoming. He looked like every woman's ideal boyfriend.

But her angry expression must have registered, because his own expression changed to one of concern as she entered his house. He lowered his hand and closed the phone, sliding it into his pocket. "Is something wrong?" he asked anxiously, shutting the door behind her.

"There certainly is!" Nicole answered. She opened the paper in front of him. "Can you explain this?"

She saw shock register on his face.

Chapter Thirteen

Jeremy stared at the newspaper Nicole held in front of him. *What did that say?* " 'TV Star's Son Launching His Own Career?' " he read, aghast.

He grabbed the paper, folding it to glance at the title. She'd been reading the *National Snoop?* Oh, no—not that publication again—it meant nothing but trouble for him and his family.

He skimmed the article, all the while his heart sinking slowly.

Oh no. Oh no. Not only was his background now exposed to Nicole—before he'd had a chance to tell her—but the article also included completely false information.

He looked up, meeting Nicole's glare, and felt his stomach—and heart and everything else inside—plummet further.

"Nicole," he said, "it's not . . . that's not . . ."

"Why didn't you tell me?" she stormed. "Why didn't you say something? Everyone else probably knows you come from a famous family, and I'm totally in the dark. You never said a word!"

Guilt and remorse stabbed him like the sharpest knife in the kitchen.

"You're right," he said, his voice raspy. "I've been figuring out how I should tell you. And if it's any consolation, I was just trying to call you for that very reason. I wanted to tell you today. I didn't want to keep it a secret any longer. Here, do you want to see my cell, see the number I was calling?" he asked, his voice rising in desperation. She looked so angry.

"No." She shook her head. "And you were using me . . ."

He interrupted. "No, that part of the article is utterly wrong! I have no TV aspirations." He ran a hand through his hair. "I've never wanted to go into acting. It was kind of fun, once in a while, to appear on a show with my mom and my brother and sisters, but I never wanted to do it more than a few times. None of us did." He took a breath. "I haven't been on *All My Relatives* for years. The last time we kids did it, it was part of a fundraiser, and we gave the money we earned for our guest appearance to a children's charity Rebecca's involved in."

"You don't want to—"

"No," he said firmly. He reached out and grabbed her shoulders. "Believe me, Nicole, I have no intentions of going into acting. I like being an electrician. And I'd never, ever use you in that way."

"Then why didn't you tell me about your family?"

Oh, no, were those tears in her eyes? His stomach twisted. The last thing he'd ever wanted to do was hurt her. He'd only wanted to protect himself. "Look," he said, steering her towards the couch. "Sit down, and I'll explain why I didn't tell you right away."

She sat stiffly on the sofa, and he sat as close to her as he dared.

"There've been a lot of girls—women—who chased after me for just that reason," he began, his heart hammering. He had to make her understand. "They were women who wanted a rich boyfriend, and women who thought my family connections could help them in their theatrical careers. The last time," he said, then stopped. Nicole still looked very angry.

"I met this woman, Monica. I thought she cared about me." He spoke slowly, willing Nicole to listen, to understand. "I thought we were falling in love. Then I overheard her one day on the phone. She didn't love me. She didn't care about me. She figured I'd introduce her to my mother, and she'd get her big break in acting, and her career would take off." He paused.

Nicole waited. Her face was still drawn, her mouth in a set line.

It was odd, he thought fleetingly. Speaking about it now, the memory didn't sting like it used to.

Was it because of his relationship with Nicole?

"Monica broke my heart," he continued. "And I vowed that would never happen again. I wouldn't let any woman take advantage of my name like that. I wasn't ever going to tell anyone about my family, not until I could be sure . . ."

Now Nicole spoke up. "But this was *me,* Jeremy! I'm not like that. I have no acting aspirations. I can see if you didn't want to tell me at first, but we've grown so close. At least, I thought we had." Her voice dwindled, becoming sad.

"We have gotten close!" he insisted.

"Not enough for you to tell me the truth," she said bitterly, shaking her head, and she did look like she was going to cry. His gut clenched. "You've had weeks to get to know me. You could have told me."

"I was going to today."

"You should have told me sooner," she went on.

"I can understand your feeling upset," he started. He inched closer, wanting badly to put his arm around her, to touch her and soothe away the hurt showing on her face, to make her understand.

She shook her head again. "You don't understand the half of it. I had a boyfriend once too, who used me like Monica used you."

That made him pause. "You did?"

"Brad came from a rich family, and he wanted someone attractive to show off," she said. "But he only intended to have a good time with me. He was going to marry a wealthy society girl. I was someone to have fun with on the side, to show off at parties and events . . ."

Jeremy's stomach twisted at her words. How could anyone even *think* of using Nicole in that way? "What a jerk," he breathed.

"You're no different!" she burst out. "You wanted to have fun with me—and get some good meals. You never trusted me, never confided in me—I was just someone—"

"Stop," he said, taking her by the shoulders. "It's not like that! Please believe me, Nicole." He searched her eyes, and when all he saw was hurt and anger, his stomach squeezed more tightly. "I didn't want to see you just for fun or meals—well, maybe at first I wanted the meals," he admitted, forcing a smile, hoping it would lighten her expression.

It didn't. "But as I got to know you, it was so much

more," he continued, dropping his voice persuasively, willing her to listen. But her posture remained stiff as she stared up at him.

"I can't believe that," she said, her voice scratchy.

"Why?" Jeremy knew he was beginning to sound desperate. "Why don't you believe me, Nicole? I only wanted to hide my identity for a little while—just to be accepted, and cared for, for *myself,* not because I came from a famous family." He frowned. "And for what it's worth, you never asked me many questions. If you had, I wouldn't have lied."

"We'll never know, will we?" she said, her voice brittle.

Now he was getting angry. "You don't trust me at all, do you?" he accused. "No, I wouldn't have lied. And you could have Googled my name, did some research. There's probably tons of info out there if you wanted . . ."

"So now it's my fault?" she snapped. "It's my fault that I didn't know?"

Too late, he realized how his words sounded—like he thought it was her fault. He swallowed. He had to take responsibility for his actions, but she was being stubborn, refusing to see his point of view. "Look," he said, "I—I'm sorry, Nicole. I should have told you earlier. I don't want this to interfere with our relationship."

"It's too late for that." She sprang up. "It's already interfered with our relationship." Her fists were balled at her side.

"It doesn't have to!" he insisted, beginning to get mad himself. "Why can't you accept what I'm saying?"

Her anger seemed to deflate in front of him. "I can't," she whispered, and turning on her heel, she hurried to the door, yanked it opened, and left.

He stared at the door.

She was going to leave—like this—despite what he thought were their growing feelings for each other? Couldn't she understand?

But inside, a very small voice was pushing at him. *Why didn't you tell her sooner? You know you should have! She deserved to know!*

He gripped a pillow.

He'd put off telling her. And now it was too late.

She practically ran back across the street, tears stinging her eyes.

Marla was waiting for her. "What happened?" she asked anxiously.

"We had a fight." Nicole paused. She had to go out. She couldn't stay home, conscious of Jeremy right across the street, aware of his comings and goings, and available if he decided to knock on her door. She needed space. "I'm going out," she said abruptly. She threw open the closet door, grabbed her old tan coat, and picked up her purse.

"Will you be all right?" Marla's expression was anxious. "I can cancel my plans with Scott and go with you."

"No, don't do that." Nicole stopped, gave her sister a hug, then added, "I'll see you later." Her throat still tight, she dashed out the door.

She could hear her cell phone ringing in her purse, but she ignored it.

She started driving, unsure where to go, and finally settled on going to the mall. She had to go somewhere, and she loved to shop, although she doubted she'd enjoy it today.

She replayed, again and again, the argument with Jeremy. How could he have deceived her? Why hadn't he told her the truth? His reason seemed flimsy. So he'd been used by someone. Hadn't he known he could trust her? She wiped away a stray tear.

Arriving at the mall twenty minutes later, she walked around. She knew she had to buy a birthday present for Kathy, and she usually started her holiday shopping early. People at the mall seemed busy and bright, rushing around with packages, laughing with friends. It only made her feel bleaker.

Her cell phone shrilled again, and she ignored it. After walking around for a few more minutes, she bought a soda and sat at a secluded table in the food court.

Peeking at her phone, she saw that both of the calls were from Jeremy. There was also a text message from Marla: CALL ME IF YOU NEED ANYTHING. She responded: THANKS.

When her phone rang again, she angrily shut it off.

She wandered around the mall, buying a few holiday candles as gifts. She couldn't find anything that struck her as right for Kathy. She stopped to eat dinner, but the constant thoughts of Jeremy and their argument made the food tasteless.

She ended at a bookstore, picking up a new cookbook she'd heard about, then decided to head home. By that time she was feeling numb, an icy coating covering her heart.

She turned on her phone just before getting into the car. She had a total of five missed calls. All were from Jeremy.

Rain began to splatter her windshield on the way home. It was after eight-thirty when she pulled into her driveway. A quick look at Jeremy's house showed it to be dark, and his Jeep was gone. Relieved, she ran up the steps and let herself into the house.

The train whistle called out, and she paused. Would she ever hear another train whistle without thinking of Jeremy and their beautiful day in the city? Had it been only a week ago? Tears pricked her eyes as she shut the door behind her.

Marla was out with Scott by now, so she had the house to herself. Dropping her coat, she carried her packages up to her room, sat on her bed, and kicked off her shoes . . . and cried.

Finally, emotionally and physically fatigued, she showered and got into her oldest, most worn flannel pajamas. Her phone was telling her she had a voice mail, and reluctantly, she listened.

It was a message from Jeremy, which he'd left over two hours ago. "We need to talk," he said. There was a pause. "I'm sorry if I hurt your feelings."

He said nothing about being sorry for what he'd done. She closed the phone with a snap.

How could he have fooled her? She had trusted him!

She left off the light in her room, not wanting him to come over and knock on the door when he came home. Maybe he'd assume she was sleeping. She was tired, but knew she couldn't sleep right now.

She took her laptop into the kitchen and made herself some soothing, decaffeinated mint tea. Then she went searching on the Internet.

Jeremy's family wasn't difficult to find.

She rapidly read article after article on entertainment news sites about his mother, his father, and their whirlwind courtship years ago. His mother had taken time off when her children were young, only appearing on TV sporadically, then had gradually gone back to working full time. The children had appeared on the show once in a while, playing her character's nieces and nephews from out of state. The audience got to see them grow up, but only occasionally. Sharon's husband Antonio had appeared only twice, as part of a special program, with the money he would have been paid going to the new wing of the hospital where he worked. And later, their children had done the same, donating any money they received for appearances to charity.

"How noble," she whispered. But deep down she knew it truly was.

She read on. Troy, the oldest, was known as the "accountant to the stars" since he worked with so many TV personalities, especially other soap opera stars. His wife was also an accountant. Sister Rebecca was an orthopedic doctor, like her father, and married to a doctor specializing in ophthalmology. Brooke was the only one in a theater-related career, scenery design, and she had been working for a college in northwest New Jersey, heading up the scenery-and-set area of their active theater department.

There wasn't much on Jeremy. Unlike his siblings, it appeared he didn't seek the limelight. There were a few notations about him graduating college with a business degree, and then a couple of articles mentioning he was self-employed.

Well, at least that confirmed that he didn't want a TV career.

She found a couple more articles. One had a photo, taken the previous winter, of the family in an airport in Colorado, on the way back from a skiing trip they'd all taken together—including Troy's young daughter. Another was an article with a photo showing Sharon and Jeremy and Brooke sightseeing in Denmark. Apparently the entire family had vacationed there a little over a year ago. The article detailed that, besides their huge house in the wealthy

Short Hills, New Jersey location, the Perez family owned a home on the coast of Florida and a luxury apartment on the Upper East Side of New York.

She should have known. She should have known. The words ran together at the back of her head, providing a drumming backdrop that was giving her a headache.

She could have looked on the Internet earlier. She could have asked around.

She rested her head in her hands. Probably half the people in this neighborhood knew. Certainly, she could have asked Mrs. Kelly. Her nosy neighbor probably knew more about Jeremy and his background than the *National Snoop* did.

Abruptly, Nicole exited the sites and shut her laptop. She got up, grabbed some of the peach cobbler, and ate in silence. A glance at the clock showed it was almost eleven. Marla and Scott would probably be back from the movies soon. She cleaned up and went upstairs, not wanting to socialize with anyone. She didn't even feel like watching *Chef vs. Chef*. It would only remind her that last Saturday they'd been at the taping of her favorite show.

Nicole got ready for bed and then lay down, refusing to look outside to see if Jeremy's car was there.

She couldn't sleep right away. Thoughts of Jeremy kept her up, despite her fatigue. Finally she heard Marla and Scott come in downstairs and felt herself drifting off.

Her last conscious thoughts were of Jeremy, and his smile . . .

Jeremy sat on the couch in the media room at his parents' house, and sighed again. He hadn't been able to concentrate on an old favorite superheroes video game. He couldn't stop thinking about Nicole.

Knowing that his parents had gone down to Atlantic City for the weekend with friends, he'd decided to escape his own home for the night and spend time at his childhood home. Though it was empty, at least he wouldn't be constantly watching Nicole's house across the street from his.

He'd tried Nicole a bunch of times, to no avail. She wasn't answering her cell phone. He knew she'd gone out, but it was after ten o'clock—she must have returned home by now, and listened to her messages at some point.

A spark of anger skimmed him. Didn't she want to talk? She was being unreasonable.

On the heels of that thought, though, came discouragement. He felt his shoulders slump. Maybe she wasn't being so unreasonable. He should have told her earlier.

Okay, he could see her being a little mad. But was it reasonable for her to be so mad she wouldn't talk to him? He just needed to explain to her, to reason with her when she had calmed down, and she would understand why he'd needed to keep his family's identity a secret.

What he really needed, he decided, was to talk to someone. But at ten-fifteen on a Saturday night, most of his friends would be either out with their wives or girlfriends; or the unattached ones would be hanging out with other friends. His sister Rebecca would be going to sleep early, tired from her pregnancy; Brooke was probably out with Will. Troy might be around though.

He called Troy, and got voice mail.

He really wanted to talk to somebody! He text-messaged Brooke, suspecting his sister was out. When he got no message after five minutes, he knew he was right.

She was probably at the movies or a party or something, most likely with Will.

He texted again: CAN WE GET TOGETHER TOMORROW? MAYBE LUNCH?

He plopped down on the deep sofa in the family room and flipped channels. He watched the news for a while, but the latest pop star scandal held no interest for him. He finally settled on a crime-investigations show that was half over. Then he found himself changing channels again.

He stopped. *Chef vs. Chef* was on. Was it only a week ago that he'd seen the live taping with Nicole? He felt an ache in his middle. Didn't she understand?

As the tablecloth was whipped off the secret ingredient— salmon—he couldn't help picturing Nicole as she'd looked last week: happy, her face glowing, her smile wide and enchanting.

He'd been so happy, so excited to be with her too.

It hit him then, like an electrical shock so strong it burned: It was love. *He loved Nicole!*

Why hadn't he realized it before? He felt like slapping himself on the forehead. He thought about Nicole all the time. He was attracted to her. He always enjoyed her company—not to mention her cooking—and wanted to be with her constantly. He wanted to please her.

He loved her.

His heart constricted and a groan escaped him. He loved her, but now he may have lost her. He should have told her the truth last week.

Was it too late now to make amends?

He dragged himself up to his old childhood room, but didn't get much sleep that night. He tossed and turned, thinking about Nicole.

By eleven o'clock in the morning he heard from Brooke, and she agreed to meet him for a late lunch. He drove towards the restaurant near her condo where they often had dinner.

"You don't look so good," she remarked as he slid into the booth.

"I don't feel so good," he admitted. "I blew it, Brooke."

She quirked her eyebrows.

"Nicole found out about our family, and now she thinks I was hiding the truth from her."

Brooke's expression turned sympathetic. "Oh, Jer," she said. She reached out and squeezed his hand. "But . . . weren't you hiding the truth?"

"No—not permanently," he protested. "I only wanted a little time."

"And you got it."

He groaned. "Ye-es," he said. "I was just about to tell her—I was calling her on the phone, for goodness' sake—and the stupid paper beat me to the punch." He explained about the *National Snoop.*

"I can understand how frustrated you feel," Brooke said carefully, seeming to weigh her words. "But think about how she feels."

He looked at his sister. "She's mad."

"And hurt, I imagine," Brooke said. "I would be. Here she is falling head over heels for you . . ."

Jeremy stared at his sister. "Do you think so?"

"I can see it in her face," Brooke asserted. "And then she finds out you're not really who she thought you were."

"It's not like I'm a criminal or anything," Jeremy protested.

"All you did was deceive her by hiding your real identity," she said dryly. "I'd be hurt and angry if it happened to me. Tell me, Jer, how would you feel if you found out Nicole came from a famous family?"

"I wouldn't care," he answered.

"Well . . . ," she said with a frown, "maybe men don't care about that stuff as much. But what if you found out that Nicole had hidden something from you—that her family was well known, say, politically—and she'd deliberately kept it from you, although a lot of other people knew?"

He thought about it. What if she did keep a secret? "I might be disturbed—but not as angry as she was."

"Remember how hurt you were that Monica was using you to get to our family for her career?" Brooke asked, her voice gentling.

The server appeared, and they paused to order. Jeremy hadn't even looked at the menu, so he simply requested a burger and fries. Brooke ordered a chicken Caesar salad.

When the server disappeared, she continued. "You were devastated that someone would use you like that—and I don't blame you. Nicole must feel the same way—devastated."

"I didn't use her," he said.

"But you hid the truth," Brooke said. She reached over and squeezed his hand, then withdrew hers when their sodas arrived. "To her, she feels used too—like you thought she wasn't important enough for you to tell her the truth."

He hadn't thought of that. "But I've always treated her well," he pointed out.

"I know!" Brooke agreed. "You're a wonderful person and a great boyfriend—except, now, she's hurt. If you had told her first, I think she would have had a different reaction. Maybe she would have been annoyed, but it wouldn't have been like this."

He nodded.

"So, the question is"—Brooke took a deep breath— "what do you want to do?"

"Do?" He stared at his sister.

"Do you want to just let her walk away, or do you want to try to mend the tear in your relationship? Do you want to fight for her?"

His insides froze. "I don't want to lose her," he said, his voice hoarse. That would be terrible. He couldn't imagine not seeing her smile, not holding her in his arms, not sharing their intimate romantic dinners. In short, he couldn't imagine life without Nicole. God, that would be awful. "I don't want to lose her," he said again, quietly.

Brooke sat back and met his eyes with her own. "So what do you think you should do?"

"I've got to apologize," he said honestly, "and I've got to make her see that we belong together."

The question was, how was he going to do that?

Chapter Fourteen

Nicole dragged herself home late Monday afternoon.

She'd managed to spend most of Sunday with her best friend from college, Ashley, who lived in Edison. Today Marla was working, so she'd gone to exercise and run a few errands before coming home. She'd hoped to get home before Jeremy so she wouldn't have to run into him, yet she dreaded going home to an empty house, with no company but her gloomy thoughts.

Jeremy had called twice yesterday, but left no messages. She hadn't felt up to speaking to him. She was still angry, and hurt, and confused. How could he have fooled her? How could she not have known? The thoughts kept bombarding her.

At the same time, she was heartbroken by the thought that their relationship might be over, that she might never see him again—except in the neighborhood.

She had no idea what she'd do about her show, but that seemed the least of her worries right now.

In the last two days she'd gotten five calls from friends

and fellow teachers who'd seen the *National Snoop* article. Everyone was curious about Jeremy, his being on the show, and their relationship. She'd tried to answer the questions evasively, implying that they were trying to keep things low-key to stay out of the media spotlight. But they hadn't, she'd said dryly, succeeded.

She was both sad and relieved to see Jeremy's car wasn't in his driveway when she pulled into hers. But she did see the blue car she recognized as Brooke's.

She closed the door after herself, dropped her purse, and went to pour a soda. She had just sat down at the kitchen table when the doorbell rang. She was tempted to ignore it, but she knew Jeremy wasn't home, so she went to answer the door.

It was Brooke. "May I come in?" she asked. Jeremy's sister looked pale, and not like her usual energetic, optimistic self.

"Uh—okay," Nicole said, uncertain of why Brooke was here.

She offered her a soda or coffee, and Brooke accepted the coffee.

While it brewed, they sat in the kitchen, and Brooke began to talk. "I know you're angry with my brother," she said without preamble. "He doesn't know I'm over here, but I wanted to speak to you. I understand why you feel like you do—I really do. But I just wanted to tell you a little about why he hid our family history from you."

"I should have known," Nicole said, running a hand through her hair. It was still damp from the shower she'd taken after exercise. "The signs were there that Jeremy came from a rich or famous family. I just didn't want to see them. And I should have," she went on. "After what I went through with my old boyfriend—well, you don't want to hear about that."

"But I do," Brooke said, her expression sincere. "Don't blame yourself. I'm actually annoyed at Jeremy for keeping it a secret for so long! I warned him you might find out and that he should come clean before that happened. But did he listen? Men," she added in a disgusted voice.

Nicole had to smile at her tone. "Yeah, men," she mimicked it. "He did tell me," she added, "that some girl used him to get to your mom."

"Yes, she had a warped idea that by getting close to Jeremy—and all of us—she could further her acting career," Brooke continued, frowning.

Nicole got up to pour the coffee for Brooke, adding milk and then sitting back down with her soda. The aroma of coffee was soothing, but she was afraid to drink it. She'd had several nights with little sleep, and she hoped by tonight she would fall asleep more easily.

"Jeremy was devastated when he found out," Brooke said, blowing on her coffee, then taking a sip. "I never saw him so upset—till yesterday. Monica really hurt him. After that, he was very suspicious of women and never told *anyone* about our background. Over and over, he said he wanted someone who cared about him for himself."

"But I do!" Nicole cried. "I lo—liked him for who he was—is. I never wanted him to be anyone but himself."

"I think he was slowly coming to realize that," Brooke said. "And I think he was going to tell you. We'd discussed it recently. I just wished he'd done it a day or two earlier."

Nicole sighed. "I wish he'd told me too. But he hid it—and yes, I know he had a reason, but he didn't trust me."

She could feel tears gathering in her eyes. "Maybe a part of him was just out to have a good time. Maybe he didn't care if I learned eventually, because then he'd just be going on to the next girlfriend . . ."

"No!" Brooke exclaimed, her face shocked. "No, Nicole—I never saw him act the way he does around you—never, not even with Monica. He adores you. That's why he put off telling you—because you mean so much to him, and he didn't want to jeopardize your relationship."

Nicole stared at Brooke. "That's hard to believe."

"Believe it." Brooke leaned forward suddenly and grasped Nicole's hand. "Nicole, I hope you think of me as a friend, as well as Jeremy's sister. I promise you, he cares. I've never ever seen him act the way he does with you. And I've never seen him so despondent as—well, since this weekend, when you had your, uh, disagreement." She blinked, and Nicole saw the sheen of tears in Brooke's eyes. "Please, please give him another chance. I know he's been calling, and I know you're upset, but you two are so wonderful together . . ."

Nicole shook her head. "It's my experience that rich guys don't want lasting relationships with average girls like me. They want to have fun with us, yes, but that's it—and then they go back to their socialite girlfriends when it's time to get serious."

"No," Brooke exclaimed, "Jeremy's not like that at all!"

"My last boyfriend was." Nicole's voice had turned bitter. "What reason do I have to believe Jeremy's going to be any different?"

"Because he is!" Brooke insisted. "I promise you. Please give him another chance."

"I don't know if he wants another chance," Nicole said, withdrawing her hand. "And I don't now if I can give him that, and trust him—even if that is what he wants."

"Just promise me you'll think about it," Brooke urged, "please?"

Nicole hesitated.

"My brother is one of the best people I know," Brooke continued. "All I'm asking is that you be open-minded and give him that chance, okay?"

Should she? She loved Jeremy. But he'd hurt her, badly. She gazed at Brooke's sincere expression and recognized how much she cared for her brother. Jeremy must be a special brother to have a sister who cared so much about him. Nicole drew a shaky breath. "I'll . . . think about it," she said slowly.

Brooke smiled. "Thank you." And she hugged Nicole.

Nicole hugged her back, clinging just a little to Jeremy's sister.

After Brooke left, Nicole felt drained and confused. She wasn't really hungry, so she made a turkey sandwich for dinner, then afterward went upstairs to her bedroom.

Was Brooke right? she kept wondering. Did Jeremy really adore her? Had she been too harsh in judging him?

She sat at her computer, about to check her e-mail, when her cell phone rang. She didn't recognize the phone number right away.

"Hello?" she said, wondering if it was a wrong number.

"Hey, Nicole!"

She sat up straight, shocked. "Is that you, Brad?" Nicole almost dropped the phone as her ex-boyfriend spoke.

"It's good to hear your voice!" he began in a jovial tone. "Hey, I see you're making a name for yourself! My friend

Derrick's wife spotted the article in the *National Snoop* about your little TV show—and your current boyfriend. Congrats, I hear he's from a nice family—famous too."

Nicole gripped the phone hard, for once speechless. What did he mean "her little TV show" and "her current boyfriend"? Before she could come up with a retort, he went on.

"I've been wondering how you are, and glad things are working out so well!" he said.

Nicole gritted her teeth. Brad sometimes had a certain tone of voice she'd taken a while to recognize. It was a self-important tone, and it set her on edge right now. "Yes, Jeremy is such a great guy. He's really the nicest guy I've ever known," she said, wondering if Brad would recognize the sarcastic edge to her voice.

"Good, good," he said enthusiastically. "Listen, Nic, I was wondering if you'd like to bring him to the hospital benefit a week from this Saturday night, to help raise money for the new cancer wing?" Brad sounded sincere, but Nicole wasn't fooled.

"Having Doctor Antonio Perez's and Sharon Maloney-Perez's son there would be great publicity for the hospital," Brad finished.

She could just picture him, with his self-important grin. "I'm sure it would be," Nicole said, as she felt herself growing hot with anger. The nerve of Brad! "But if I wasn't good enough for you a couple of years ago, why would I be now? You only want me there because I'm dating someone famous."

"Now, Nic—"

She interrupted him. "Don't deny it, Brad. I'm not good enough to date seriously, but I'm good enough to invite along with someone *you* want to show off."

"It's not like that at all—"

"Sorry, we're busy that night." She took a deep breath, forcing herself to get calmer and cooler. "We're going to an event where I'm wanted for myself, and not looked at as a second-class citizen tagging along with the real guest."

He made a protesting noise.

"Good-bye, Brad." Very coolly, she shut her phone and ended the call.

She stared at the phone. Instead of thinking about Brad, she was picturing Jeremy. Jeremy had never made her feel like a second-class citizen. He'd always made her feel like her company was wanted, for herself. And suddenly she knew. She knew how Jeremy felt.

He had felt the way she was feeling now—wanted only for her connection to someone famous, wanted not because she was a desired friend or even an outstanding citizen, wanted simply because of her connections to someone else.

It was a distasteful feeling.

No wonder Jeremy had been so upset with his old girlfriend. She'd used him, and it wasn't pretty. Nicole had simply been approached with a similar scenario and it made her stomach turn. As loathsome as it was for her, it must have been a hundred times worse for Jeremy, who had been fooled and used for his family connections.

For the first time, she could really understand why he'd kept his family connections hidden.

On the heels of that thought came consternation. She'd been hurt and angry, and she'd lashed out at Jeremy. She'd ignored his calls. "Oh, no," she whispered. "What have I done?" She put her head in her hands.

Had she totally lost Jeremy—the man she loved, the man who had always treated her well?

A sob escaped her. What had she done? And what could she do to make it right?

Her grandmother's words echoed in her mind. *The way to a man's heart is through his stomach.*

And suddenly she knew what she could do.

Chapter Fifteen

On Tuesday, Nicole stayed at school late for her cooking club, then went to the grocery store and bought ingredients to make lasagna.

That was the dinner she'd made first for Jeremy, and it seemed to be one of his favorites. He had spoken about it often.

She'd decided that the best way to apologize to Jeremy was face-to-face—with food. "The way to a man's heart is through his stomach," she whispered to herself.

She knew he had dinner on Tuesdays with Brooke, and she had been tempted to call Brooke and ask her to change that. After debating it with herself last night, she'd picked up the phone and asked Brooke exactly that.

"I think making him dinner is a great idea," Brooke said enthusiastically. "But . . . uhm . . . if I cancel our Tuesday dinner, Jeremy might get suspicious."

"Oh, you're right." Disappointment pierced Nicole. "Okay, I guess I'll plan the dinner for Wednesday."

"That might be best," Brooke said in a soothing tone. "And . . . I'm glad you want to make up with him, Nicole."

"I do. More than anything." Her throat was tight as she finished, "I love your brother. He's the best man I've ever met."

"I'm so glad," Brooke responded. "I think you're perfect for each other. I'll keep my fingers crossed that everything works out."

Nicole had called Marla's cell phone next, knowing that she would check it when she had her dinner or snack break. She briefly told her what she was planning.

Sure enough, Marla had called back around eight o'clock. "Great idea," Marla had said. "The way to a man's heart is through his stomach and all that—although, Nicole, he loves you for yourself, not for your cooking. I'm positive of it."

"Thanks for that. Since Wednesday is your day off this week . . . do you mind making yourself scarce?"

"Not at all," her sister had answered promptly. She'd sounded slightly amused. "I have a feeling things will work out."

"I hope so." Nicole was trying to be optimistic. "Listen, you'll never guess who called me, and made me realize just how wonderful Jeremy is!" She'd proceeded to tell her sister about Brad's call.

Marla had been astonished. After a few minutes, Marla had said, "Listen, Nic, I have to get going. Someone delivered triplets a couple of hours ago, and we've been really busy. I have to eat and get back on the floor."

When Nicole had hung up, she'd felt better. Marla was a great sister and friend, and she liked Brooke a lot too. She was a friend too—and maybe, someday, she'd be a sister-in-law.

She'd gone to the window and gazed out at the sliver of moon and the dark night. Maybe, maybe . . . she could hope . . .

She'd had most of the ingredients she needed in the house, except for the lasagna noodles and ricotta cheese. She'd stopped quickly at the store for those things after her cooking club was finished.

As she exited her car now, she glanced at Jeremy's house, which had become a habit. She was surprised to see that his van was there. It was only four-thirty. Maybe he'd finished up work early today and come home before meeting Brooke.

The day had started sunny but turned cloudy, and she was beginning to feel discouragement as she went up the sidewalk, holding her purse and grocery bag. What if Jeremy felt he was finished with their relationship? It would break her heart.

And she knew then that her relationship with Brad had been a caring one, but nothing like what she felt for Jeremy—nothing like this. This was true love.

He had to give her another chance. He had to . . .

She turned the key and pushed the front door open.

The smell of something burnt greeted her.

Panic hit her. Something was burning? But as she sniffed again, it smelled like—like something baked. Had Marla left something in the oven too long, and the smell hadn't disappeared yet? Her sister rarely burned anything, though. Marla was working today—her car was gone. But a burnt smell might linger for hours.

She found herself calling out "Marla?" anyway as she shut the door and took a step forward. With a few more breaths she thought she could identify it: corn bread.

Someone was burning corn bread in her kitchen?

She dropped her bag and purse on the dining room table, which was set with two place settings—dishes, utensils, and wineglasses. In the middle stood a large jar candle she'd bought a few weeks ago and hadn't used yet. It was pumpkin pie-scented and unlit. She'd left it in the kitchen when she'd bought it. The rather haphazard table setting didn't look like Marla's work.

She went towards the kitchen. The light was on, and she heard something clink. "Marla?" she asked again.

Jeremy appeared in the doorway.

Nicole stared at Jeremy. He looked tired, his expression uncertain. He had a dark shadow on his face, and his long-sleeved dark green T-shirt had a splotch of sauce on it.

But he'd never looked so good.

"Jeremy?" She stepped forward, beginning to shake. Was he cooking in her kitchen? She could smell meat, and spices—was that chili?

"Nicole—I—" he said and stopped.

Suddenly she felt her mouth turning upwards. "Are you cooking?" Her heartbeat was rapid, and she took a step closer to get a glimpse of the kitchen. The smell of burnt corn bread was stronger here. Ah, she was right, she thought as she spotted it on the counter, the top of the corn bread brown instead of golden. A large pan on the stove appeared to hold simmering chili. There were several splatters of sauce surrounding it.

She turned back to Jeremy, raising her eyes to look at him. "Jeremy?" Her voice was shaking too.

His green eyes regarded her seriously, and he shoved his hands into his jeans pockets. "You said it would be wonderful if I cooked dinner for you." His voice was hoarse, his expression serious. "I wanted to do something wonderful. I made you dinner, Nicole."

"Oh, Jeremy," she whispered, and placed her shaking hand on his cheek. "I—you made me dinner—by yourself?"

"Yes," he answered, his eyes never leaving hers.

"Oh, Jeremy!" she exclaimed and flung her arms around him.

He held her tightly, and she felt tears roll down her cheeks.

"You made me dinner," she said around the lump in her throat.

"Because I'm sorry, Nicole." He tightened his grip. "I never meant to hurt you. I should have told you about my family sooner, but I was afraid . . ."

She pulled back enough to see his beloved face. "I realized last night just how you felt—how it feels to have someone use you for your connections. I'll tell you about it later but—I finally knew how you felt. I'm sorry, Jeremy. I should have been more understanding."

"No, you were right. I was inconsiderate."

"No, you're the most considerate man I know." She touched his cheek with a still-trembling hand.

"You're the best person I've ever met." He said it solemnly. "And I swear to you, Nicole, I'll always consider your feelings from now on. I was thinking only about myself. I was selfish and I'm sorry. Can you forgive me?"

"We'll have to forgive each other," she said, her heart now beating with gladness.

"Good, because I won't forgive myself until you forgive me." He waved at her kitchen and the food contained there. "I thought this would be the best way to show you how much I loved you. And I do, Nicole." His gaze locked with hers. "I love you very much."

Jeremy loved her!

"I love you too!" she cried, and then she was engulfed in his arms again, and he was kissing her and she was kissing him back until they were both breathless.

A sudden hissing made her pull back. "I think the chili might be burning."

"Yikes, I burnt the corn bread too, I'm afraid."

They both made a dash for the stove, and Jeremy turned it off while Nicole moved the pan. Then they turned to each other, and burst out laughing.

"You remembered how to cook this from my show?" she asked.

"I remembered some of it. I had to call Marla and review the recipe. And she let me in before she left for work."

"Oh, and I brought the ingredients home to make *you* dinner," Nicole said, picking up the grocery bag from the table. "I was going to make you dinner tomorrow since I thought you were out with Brooke tonight. I even called Brooke and told her."

"I cancelled." He grinned, his eyes now sparkling. "She must have realized when you called that we both had the same plan. She didn't say anything to me."

"She didn't say anything to me, either. She must be getting a laugh out of this." Nicole surveyed the kitchen, which looked a little worse for wear. "I'll bet this is going to be the best meal I ever ate."

Jeremy laughed. "Yeah, it'll be my very own version of *A Taste of Romance.*"

Epilogue

The show, two weeks later

And now our chicken cacciatore is ready," Nicole said, beaming at the camera. "And so is our pasta."

"I'll take that," Jeremy said, smiling, and lifted the bowl.

They moved to the table. Jeremy had called earlier and said he'd had a job near the cable station and would meet her there. She'd been surprised to find he'd already set the table for their romantic dinner.

"You're doing most of the cooking," he'd said in a good-natured voice. "I don't mind setting the table."

Now, the camera zoomed in on the picturesque table setting, complete with an autumnal tablecloth and gold-colored, thick cloth napkins. The wineglasses had a gold rim and the candle holders were white and gold.

"I'll bet it's going to taste as good as it looks," Jeremy said, placing his napkin on his lap.

Nicole lifted her napkin, and a small box clattered out onto the table.

"What's this?" she asked, staring at it. It was covered in

dark blue satin—a jeweler's box. Suddenly, her heart started pounding. She raised her eyes to meet Jeremy's.

He was smiling at her. "Open it," he urged.

Nicole's hands shook as she picked up the box and pried it open. Inside, a large oval-shaped diamond glowed with dazzling light.

She gasped, and suddenly Jeremy was kneeling beside her, holding her hand.

"Nicole," he said. His voice had turned solemn. "I love you. I know I always will. I want to share all my meals with you—breakfast, lunch, and dinner, not just romantic dinners. I want to share more than that. I want to share our lives." His green eyes gleamed. "Will you marry me?"

"Oh, Jeremy—yes!" Nicole cried, and then they were in each other's arms, hugging and kissing and laughing.

Jeremy pulled back after a minute, took the ring from the box, and slid it on Nicole's finger.

"A taste of romance is not enough," he said, grinning. "I want a lifetime."

"I do too," she said, smiling up at the man she loved.

They kissed again. Somewhere nearby she vaguely heard someone say "Cut!" in an amused voice.

But neither Nicole nor Jeremy cared. They were too busy kissing and sharing their taste of romance and true love!